The One Percenters

By

John W. Podgursky

Damnation Books, LLC.
P.O. Box 3931
Santa Rosa, CA 95402-9998
www.damnationbooks.com

The One Percenters
by John W. Podgursky
Digital ISBN: 978-1-61572-013-2
Print ISBN: 978-1-61572-012-5

Cover art by: Daniele Serra
Edited by: Heather Williams
Copyright 2009 John W. Podgursky

Printed in the United States of America
Worldwide Electronic & Digital Rights
1st North American & 1st UK Print Rights

Dedicated to
My mother, for her unyielding support.

Acknowledgements:
I wish to thank the people who make me feel
semi-normal. You know who you are.

Chapter One

My mother used to say I have a tendency to dwell on the subject of death. I tend to disagree with the bitch. I don't dwell; I savor. Here's why:

Her name was Samantha James. An all-American name for an all-American girl. She was born just before the Zeldas, Phoebes and Zoes inherited the Earth—back when there remained a small measure of sense to life. Before the pixie dust of the new millennium stole our innocence. Sam worked as a checkout girl at the market on Fifth, and we met on a rainy morning that now feels like a lifetime ago.

I won't get bogged down in tedious detail; there's no need to make it messy. Samantha was methodical in her daily schedule, a fact that made for simple timing on my part. And timing is essential in matters such as these. I waited beside the dumpster until she exited the grocery on her lunch break, and together we made for the woods, though she needed a little prodding. I understood that. We would take it slowly, one step at a time. It was best that way.

I had packed what little I possessed into two neatly tied plastic bags, knowing I would soon be on the move again. It was not my intention to befriend Sam for long. I needed only to spill my guts, to regain my sense of dignity. I lost that back at the lake when the screams echoed in my ears.

Sam's entrance into my life was far from random. Young, bright, and beautiful, she represented the naiveté and denial running rampant in the world today. It would be easy to convince someone of my own grain; I would be preaching to the choir. Rather, I felt I needed a new and different challenge. Sam would have to do. She was a pretty doll indeed.

It was midday when I began my discourse. The rain had tapered, though the sky was still a hostile gray. There was no noise in the forest at that time, which is unusual. Forests are full of buzzes, whistles and hums.

Sam stood facing me, tied to a tree, whimpering from behind the bandana. This hurt me. I didn't want to see pain on her face. Who would? I had seen and experienced enough pain in my lifetime to that point. I only needed her to listen, to be my friend for a while. I hadn't had many friends.

Her sadness seemed decidedly ironic. Here I was, trying to let her in on perhaps the most important process in the world around her, rescuing her from a few hours of mindless and unfulfilling labor, and she was in tears. She should have been rejoicing to the heavens!

As Sam stood before me tied to that tree, she was shaking noticeably. I suppose I can't blame her. There is, after all, no magic pill I could give her to show her what kind of a man I was. There is no quick trust in this lifetime. You can't fake time spent. Whatever I wanted to instill in her had to come through the spoken word, and what better and more natural form of expression is there than systematic grunting?

I removed the gag from her mouth, slowly and with an expression that made it plain she was to maintain her composure. Even if she was to be trusted, I could not trust the world at large to understand. Not yet, and probably never.

"Samantha."

There was no response from her. I tried repeatedly to elicit an answer, but did not wish to resort to violence. I was out to help, not to hurt.

"Samantha."

Still nothing. Fine then. I would wait. I am, after all, a patient man. It's a gift, I know. Some folks must learn patience, slowly and with great frustration.

An hour passed, and she cried a lot.

Tears are funny; their calming effect. Crying stabilizes. I knew it was only a matter of time before Sam came to her senses. I was right, and she did. At last, she motioned awkwardly at me with her head. She was free to speak, but was apparently uncomfortable in doing so. I edged closer to her. Finally:

"What do you want?" Her words were weak and choked upon. They came out as one long, forced word.

I'd been rehearsing my response all morning.

"I only require you listen. I am not here to hurt you. In fact, if I knew you better, we could be having this conversation right in front of the market. Although it is quite beautiful out here, wouldn't you say?" Forest aesthetics— humble, splendid, even eerie—are among my favorite.

Again it took her a long time to respond.

"H-How do you know my name?"

"I've been watching you, and I asked around a bit. The details aren't important, really." Indeed they weren't. Details are for the compulsive, the anxious-minded. I had learned that from years in the advertising business. Go with the flow.

Suffice it to say we spoke for a while that day in the woods on Fifth Street. In the end, she asked me:

"What are you going to do to me?"

The inevitable question. I didn't immediately answer.

When we met in the parking lot that morning, I had hoped that Sam would turn out to be one of *them*. It would have made this so much easier for me— two birds with one stone and all that. After our little therapeutic dialogue in the forest, she would help me in my mission, passively. I thought I could do it without so much as batting an eyelash, just as I had the other times. But it wasn't turning out that way. In the course of our discussion that day, I sensed a big heart within her. I sensed passion and wit, and strength. These are rare assets. I hadn't planned for this discovery, and in truth, I wasn't sure I could answer her question yet. I didn't know *what* I was going to do with her.

How had it all come to this? I only know how it began.

Chapter Two

I found her body on a Tuesday; that much I remember. I had been infatuated with Jill from the start, and in the end, we had shared the type of selfless, warm love that perhaps one in ten will encounter in their miserable, self-centered lives. Then, she was no more than a cooling corpse at the edge of the woods. Her eyes were half-shut, which of course means they were also half-open. I didn't feel comfortable closing the world off to them for the last time, so I sat there under her creepy gaze. I felt for a few moments like she would spring up from the ground with a sharp "Boo!" and it would all be over. It would mean that my nightmare would never have started, and I'd be sleeping much more comfortably these days, unaware of what I now know. Sometimes it's better we don't know.

It was raining cold upon her form, and there was leaf litter in her hair. In a state of combined shock and grief, I picked the leaves out and covered her with my coat, shielding her body from the weather, preserving her dignity. Dignity was all I could grant her now; someone had assured that. Some *man*.

The articles in all the papers opened with Jill's name, but after the initial courtesy mention, she was known simply as Number Seven. Lucky number seven. My Jill was one of the eventual nine struck down by the Solemn Stalker in the autumn of '05. His calling card was one small Bible placed alongside each of his victims. I've always wondered if perhaps it was a sign of a strong sense of irony. I know now that it was indeed a "he," though I had assumed it from the start. Jill's panties were in the down position upon my arrival on the scene.

The late-night talk show hosts had a feast joking about this guy. Originally, I found myself laughing right along with them, but a situation seems very different indeed, when it affects you personally. Perspective becomes skewed. After Jill died, I was hoping someone would knock off the comedians. Maybe they'd die laughing, if you'll pardon the hackneyed pun. Laughter comes hard for me these days, like breath after a blow to the sternum.

I will say this: you have to be pretty good to kill nine women in three months, and pretty angry too. Having thought it over, I didn't buy the insanity bit—the excuse eventually given by the Solemn Stalker (even while maintaining his innocence!). There are mutations and fuck-ups in nature to be sure—I've met plenty of them—but insanity is a little too convenient for my liking. As far as I'm concerned, anyone who is both calculating enough to kill, and cognizant enough to get off on the sick power trip rape provides him, is all too aware of what's going on. Cuckoo people don't give a shit about power. They have enough on their minds.

Jill was wearing a white sweater when her throat was cut. I remember the blood showing up well on it. There was a lot, as you would imagine, although I suspect it wasn't quite as bad as my mind remembers. These things always look much worse when clothing becomes bloodstained. Her sweater looked like it had been washed along with several dozen tubes of lipstick—the color all the neo-bimbos wore those days.

They found her killer a month (and two murders) later. Jeffrey Simons was his name—the name of an accountant, not a felon. I thought that then, and I think it now. He was a short guy, wiry and bearded. Stable background, loving family. Worked as a bartender, and was well liked by folks at his restaurant of employ. He even hosted an annual holiday party for his coworkers. How nice. This was the man who stole my life and my happiness. Apparently he just snapped. That's the best the so-called experts could do. We think we're so damn smart, we *H. Sapiens* do. We pretend to have it all figured out. I guess we all just want to feel in control, like Jeff Simons.

I saved the news clippings for a while, but tossed them in protest of the glorification they provided this guy. Some things are not worth remembering. Now I just cry in memory. Yes, even now. Some man *I* am.

I was happy they found him, but I suppose that much is obvious. Besides providing closure, it got the police off my case and out of my life. Cops are generally good people, and certainly necessary for society to function (such as it does). But if you don't need to encounter one for a good long while, chances are your life is going okay.

Other people came calling, too. You wouldn't believe the attention you get when a serial killer bumps off your wife. Not just friends and family, but media, book publishers, religious zealots, psychiatrists. The world is full of people with little taste and less class. I guess we can't all be like my Jill. She made up for my many flaws and then some. And that's saying a lot, I assure you.

I now know what empty feels like. Empty is eating the last cookie in the box. Suddenly it's gone, and you're not sure you'll ever get out to the store again. You're left with memories of the chocolate flavor, but your stomach is soon growling again, and that's all that really matters. I wanted my wife back. Get your own damn wife, Jeffrey!

I wanted to drive to the prison and slay him with my own hands, but that's not the right thing to do, is it. I suppose I should have moved, right there and then, to a state that has the death penalty, just in case lightning should strike twice. But I didn't.

I said earlier that you have to be good to commit nine murders. As it turned out, Simons was downright lucky as well. According to the newspapers, he left quite a trail and the cops had a good idea of the murderer's profile after Number Three bought the farm (a fat accountant by the name of Mary Peters).

When they apprehended Simons, there was some controversy concerning the length of time it had taken to pinpoint the culprit. Considering the death spree lasted barely three months, there must have been a hell of a lot of misread evidence in the early cases for anyone to complain about "find-time," as the papers labeled it. I'm not a detective, but I think three months is pretty damn good. These things often stretch out over years and involve the cooperation of several precincts.

Personally, I think the media was disappointed at having lost a hot scoop so quickly. Their questioning of police method was probably just a desperate attempt to rekindle public interest in the case.

In the end, though, they had such an abundance of evidence against Simons for murders one through five that the rest became an afterthought. Come to think of it, the police didn't spend all that much time at the site of Jill's murder— or so I've heard—and hardly appeared the meticulous group of investigators one views on late-night "real detective" shows. I guess six through nine were just tack-on sentences in the pragmatic minds of the cops.

Nine murders. I remember thinking *at least the guy got his money's worth before he was caught.* I know that sounds insensitive, especially considering my closeness to the case, but sometimes you have to laugh to keep from crying.

It's funny, the things that crossed my mind those days. Shock can do funny things to a man's thinking. I guess it's a physical defense. If you don't buy that theory, drink water and shit ice, because you are one cold fucker. Anyway, I don't remember asking your opinion.

I took to drinking after Jill's murder. I had always been a wine guy, zinfandel and then merlot as I aged, but I found myself holding the whiskey bottle on a daily basis. It gets the job done quicker, and it doesn't leave that nappy feeling in your throat if you overindulge, which I did frequently. Alcohol can be your best friend. A draining and dangerous friend, though, the one who is constantly borrowing money and secretly banging your wife on the side. You don't admit it to yourself, but you know what's going on. You keep quiet, of course, as long as he keeps making you feel oh so good—keeps making you forget.

My mailman started delivering the mail to my door. I know that he meant well by it. He was a nice man who walked with a limp on the left side. His name was Tom Jefferson—I kid you not. He was a tall man with one of those brushy mustaches that is so full, it interferes with the bearer's speech and makes him sound like he's speaking through a towel.

Tom would come to the door, junk mail and solicitations in hand, and greet me with a courteous though not overly cheerful, "Afternoon, Mr. Caine."

I'd just nod my head and reach for the mail through my torn screen door. I wish I had Jill's gun when that mutt tore through the screen. Tom would go on and on for a while. One afternoon, I invited Tom in and served him coffee. As he drank, I said nothing and let him small-talk away. Eventually he ran out of comments on the weather, and we sat there in awkward silence.

The very next day, my mail started coming to the box again. I guess he took the hint. It was worth a cup of coffee. Tom's all right as acquaintances go, but he lives by too many rules, it's a cinch to tell. His shirt was always over starched, and I never heard him use a contraction. It was always "It is" and "Can not" and "We have." Silly man. I wanted to stick a catalogue up his ass. The big one with all the riding mowers and circular saws. Just the one I imagine he most hates delivering.

I quit work too. I don't think I've mentioned that. I quit work and watched an awful lot of TV. I think I missed conversation. I watched a lot of soap operas, which I suppose must seem a rather strange thing for a grown man to admit. I suppose I just enjoyed seeing people in relationships, even if those relationships were based on shallow, wanton desires. Besides, people on soaps are always pretty, and it felt good to look at pretty faces and asses. Whom are we kidding with this equal opportunity bullshit? Anybody seen by the public should have to pass some type of beauty test. Who wants to be served a burger by some hairy woman with a mustache like Tom's?

Jill had a very pretty face. I always told her that it reflected her soul so that the whole world would know what a saint she was. Her eyes could only be compared—favorably—to the bubbles that accumulate on the top layer of a bucket of sudsy water—reflective, sparkling, almost iridescent. Her eyes were blue centered with green trim. Deep, honest and thoughtful, they whispered "believe." But that means fuck-all now.

Most of the time I was depressed and in an alcoholic stupor. It's a hell of a mix. I looked like a caricature of a drunk—stubbly face, white undershirt, matted hair—and I certainly played the part well.

I woke up on the couch one morning with crumbs in my ears. I started to get minor bedsores, and realized if I didn't get up off that damn sofa, I was gonna be in a world of pain. I kept one of the empty whiskey bottles as a reminder never to let myself get into that state of mind again. For a while, it worked. For a while.

After Jill died, I realized there wasn't much depth to my life. I had few friends and fewer hobbies. What can I say? Jill was my whole world. I was never very popular in school, and after I found her, I figured my luck-well had been tapped clean. Besides, I didn't need anybody else. I like to think that Jill felt the same way. All the same, she had plenty of friends. Women who look like her and act like her and think like her usually do.

She tried to acquaint me with them on several occasions so that we could all go out as a unit, but I resisted. I felt they were *her* friends, *her* independence. She didn't need me horning in on that out of self-pity. There's nothing worse than a slob husband who leeches onto his wife's social life.

There was another reason I kept my distance. One of her friends in particular was especially attractive. Jessica Solsberg. Jessicas are almost always beautiful—kind of like the anti-Marge. Miss Solsberg is the only woman I can recall ever looking at with a sexual eye after I met Jill. It wasn't intentional, and of course I would *never* have fooled around with her or anyone else. I knew what I had in my wife. Mine was the one for which that Commandment was written.

Jill had Jess over occasionally to tan in the yard. Jessica would wear a turquoise bikini—always the turquoise bikini. Jill wore red. I made sure I happened to be repairing the roof or mowing the lawn or otherwise engaged outdoors on those days. Hey, you can't blame me for being a man. Jill was the angel, not me. Yin, yang, right? Anyway, I never cheated on her, like I said—not so much as a kiss or a pat on the bottom.

If I had been married to Jessica, you can bet shine-to-shit that I'd have been checking out Jill from head to ass. Just a natural thing is all, the desire to kiss, to touch, and to tie up. But, hell, I don't have to explain myself to anyone, especially you, Doctor. And it felt good to get the tingles when I saw Jess laying out. Turquoise still warms my loins.

I experimented with suicide. I downed a few pills, but I knew they wouldn't be enough to do the trick. I tried the razor routine, but couldn't bring myself to break the skin. In the end, I found that I'm not very good at committing suicide. If I had really meant it, I suppose I'd have gone straight for the gun, but it's not as easy as you might think. You have to give those people a certain credit for their persistence.

Death is one hell of a scary concept. You have to be hurting pretty badly to off yourself, especially if you believe in a heaven-and-hell type god. I happen not to. Funny... I feel I almost have to offer an apology for that. "Atheist" is right up there with "terrorist" in our society. Mother used to tell me that a religion is a cult dressed in a pretty little hat.

Anyway, God—or at least the belief in Him—wasn't what stopped me; I just got yellow. Besides, I didn't think it right that I should die before Mr. Simons. Thinking of that made me want to live to see the man rot away. Rot. A. Way.

I kept myself in excellent shape for a bit after my suicide adventures, trying to up my life force to outlive him—one of the stages of murder recovery, I suppose. I toned my muscles up nicely, and my back seemed to straighten itself without my effort. Eventually, though, I slipped backwards and gained twenty pounds to the fifteen I had lost. In the end, I regained my love for cheeseburgers. Life is all about progress and regression, and when the former loses out to the latter, you can be sure that before too long, birds will be using your headstone for a hopper. We are all carcasses waiting to happen, and that's strangely reassuring to me.

I wish I could tell you that my meeting Jill came at a dramatic moment—changing her tire in the rain, an encounter at the Grand Canyon, etc. Sorry to say, it didn't. Life rarely works the way the movies make it seem.

She was wearing a fuzzy, orange shirt. It had a V-neck and ran all the way down to her thighs. Man, did she look incredible. We were in a stationery store; I had gone in for cigarettes. I later gave up smoking altogether (for a while), but at that point in time, I hadn't even worked my way down to lights. Giving up cigarettes is a lot like giving up eating or breathing, or like losing your best friend. You feel like you'll die if you don't get another drag, and sooner or later you become jealous of everybody you see with a butt in their hand.

Dangerous as smoking is, the chances that *any one* smoker will die from it are not all that great, considering. So there they stand, those damn smokers, puffing away, most likely without retaliatory measures awaiting from the man in the black cloak. And you get very jealous. Most especially, you get jealous of smoking athletes. These people smoke a pack-plus daily and still run six-minute miles like nobody's business. I mean, what's *that* about? I halfway hope to develop diabetes or something like that just so I can smoke and smoke and smoke to my heart's content. You can't die twice, and you only live once.

Jill was standing in the card aisle looking at Mother's Day cards. I was on my way out when I noticed her. I was twenty-two, and had never before approached a woman I didn't know. Most of my dates had come as a result of friendships gone awry. Something was different in this case though. I'm not saying it was love at first sight; I don't believe in such a thing. That's just the groin talking.

Anyway, it wasn't love at first sight. It wasn't a psychic thing or an issue of fate. I'm also not a new-ager. I don't name my pets after minerals. I just felt from a practical standpoint that should I get rejected, I could quietly walk away and never see her again. I guess I had never realized that before. Up to that time, I always felt that women held all the power in this life. Ah, let's face it, they do.

I just walked over to her and said, "Mother's Day. The cards come out earlier every year."

Certainly not the wittiest or most profound comment, but it broke the ice, and hey, I was nervous, so fuck off.

"I suppose they do."

I tried several other openings, but each elicited a similarly curt reply. At the time I thought she was playing the part of a cautiously standoffish woman. I later found out that her mother died when Jill was young. Jill looked at the cards to live vicariously, if only for a moment, and she had been reminiscing when I approached. Her distraction was understandable; I hear her mom was a terrific woman.

"I'm sorry to bother you, really I am. It's just that I'm new to the city and I don't know anybody here. I need someone to show me around, and I...was hoping you might do that."

I was afraid of her reaction, and took the desperate and pathetic route.

"I'd pay you, of course."

Not my finest moment, certainly, but I hoped to sound disarming.

After a brief question/answer period, and to my utter shock, she agreed to my request. (No payment necessary, of course.) I don't guess I came off as a particularly threatening man. I don't guess I ever did. Samantha might disagree, out there in the forest.

We hit it off. Jill admired my honesty and openness, and we had our first kiss on Farmer's Bridge, down by the lake. We married nine months later. Very quick for people so young, I'm aware, but we knew it was right. We always knew. It was a small wedding, and my brother was my best man. We're not especially close, but I felt it only right. This was before he found the love of *his* life—her initials are P.C.P. My dad's not in the picture; I'll leave it at that.

So we walked the aisle on a very pleasant day, and thus began a lifetime of utter bliss. Until that prick took her from me.

It should have been someone else. My eighth grade teacher was a real conservative, volatile fuck—the type to send you to the principal's office if you showed up twelve seconds late, even if your pancreas hung out of your ass. It should have been *his* wife who was slaughtered. He deserved it, not me. People like him—assholes—never get the bad stuff. They just keep on... existing so they can pull the rug out from under another misguided child. Little viruses they are. Repugnant, vile parasites condemned to miserable lives.

Edwards—that was his name—had a real skinny wife. She'd meet him down at the school each afternoon. If they'd been fanciful, carefree people, I'd presume it was so they could go fuck somewhere and reaffirm their eternal, undying love. Not these two, though. A couple of heartless, soulless, gutless Antichrists. God knows she should have had her throat cut. I might do it for her. Now that I consider, she's probably already dead. I can't help but smile, though I promise you it's a small smile.

I remember feeling tremendously lonely during my drunken stage—not just for the love a woman provides, but for basic human companionship. Loneliness comes and goes with your situation in life, and nobody likes it. You show me a happy loner, and I'll show you an attractive scrotum.

The actual feeling of being alone is not so bad. With a few beers and a good western flick, you can shake it off. At times, you feel lucky not to have someone nagging you at every commercial break. The real horror is the vulnerability you assume. People who are lonely can be exploited for favors and for money. The lonelier you feel, the harder you try to dig out of the hole, often spending too much money and getting yourself into awkward or even dangerous situations. Believe me, I know. Before I was married, I was beaten and robbed at a bar by some girl with an attitude. By a *girl*. She wasn't a brute or anything. She caught me from behind, and her hand was packed with something, I'm sure. So I know what loneliness can breed.

I know all too well.

Chapter Three

I started to crave conversation. I ran out to the curb to get my mail, but Tom was no sucker, and after the coffee incident, our conversations were brief and cold. I can't say I blame him. Tommy Jefferson. Poor bastard had a lot to live up to. Might as well name your kid Christ or some such.

I began to go out in an effort to make friends, something I hadn't tried to do since high school. I discovered something very interesting: there are a lot of pricks out there. A lot of people who aren't very interesting, as well. Once in a while you find a good apple, but usually they have busy lives and your relationship with them ends when one of you walks out of the bar, or stumbles out, depending on just how good a conversation we're talking about.

I remember one night in particular when I walked spontaneously into a Goth bar. I must admit, I loved the atmosphere. Plenty of black curtains, red candles, dried wax, and circular glass tables. Music was piped in at immeasurable volume. It was dark, depressing, and at times downright scary. If it were possible to smell heroin from five feet, I would have keeled over, I'm sure. The place was filled with potential nodders. Axioms (as the bar was called) was also rather interesting. There were some good freaks there with all the piercings, tats, and zoned-out looks. I highly recommend going to one of these places at least once in your life, especially if you don't consider yourself the type. Just be sure to take an open mind. A can of mace wouldn't hurt either.

I was feeling rather lonely and sad that night. I met a tall blonde named Alisha who had an expression on her face to match my own. We talked at the bar for two hours, and we must have been quite remarkable sight—a thirty-something guy in a cheap suit talking to a twenty-two year old girl with streaks of blue in her hair and multiple piercings. Anyway, it turned out that she was going through a rough patch in her life as well.

She was originally from Jersey, but her parents had kicked her out when she was eighteen; apparently they had never seen eye to eye. After struggling by herself in the East Coast grind, Alisha made her way out here. She had run out of money six months earlier, and had lived on the streets until taking a job six weeks prior to our meeting. She wanted to go home to her friends (she still had no use for her family), but that was 2,000 miles and many bad memories away. We've all heard the story before. Thankfully, most of us haven't lived it.

The conversation did wonders for our moods, and the liquor did wonders for our sex drives. We ended up screwing in the club's ladies' room. Somehow I don't think I was her first. Despite the fact that I was still in mourning for Jill, I didn't feel an ounce of guilt at the time, and I certainly don't now. Sex is sex. I don't imagine I was any good, though—drunk, tired, and out of practice.

It's funny what you remember. The stall we were in was filthy with graffiti. Mostly it was just "I was here" and the "Jeff sucks dick" kind of stuff, but there was one message I remember well. On the door in black ink was scrawled "It's too late for Linda." I had no idea who Linda was, but I sure hope it turned out okay for her. A lot of lonely people live and die on the doors of bathroom stalls.

I stuck a twenty in Alisha's purse when she wasn't looking. I wanted to help, but didn't want her feeling like a whore. Maybe she did anyway. Oh, well, at least she wouldn't be a hungry whore. Not that night.

I got myself involved in a once-a-week poker match. I had played some with my dad, the asshole, as a lad, and I remembered loving it. That had been a long time ago, though, so I bought myself a refresher book. I found an ad in the classifieds looking for a fourth. Three losers, no doubt, looking for a fourth. I was their man. The next weekend, I showed up at a ranch that had some of the most spectacular landscaping I'd ever seen. Turned out the homeowner was a horticulturist. Not a bad person to know on the "got pull" scale. If there's one thing to remember in life, it's this: make friends with a carpenter, a dentist, and an attorney. There's nary a crisis one of those three gents can't fix, and free is damn cheap, if you get my drift.

Three loser friends greeted me at the door: Don, Terry, and Reynolds. I don't know if Reynolds was his first or last name; I didn't care, so I didn't bother to ask. We were at his house and I remember it smelled of cheese.

I played okay and actually came out a few dollars ahead, but I was bored out of my skull. I guess poker's not really about the cards, but the company. That's why solitaire is the finest game: you get to spend some quality time with your best friend.

Anyway, there I was with three idiots who were sitting around talking about the nagging tendencies of their wives. That was not my idea of a good time, especially as my own wife was currently serving as a soup kitchen for earthworms and earwigs. One of the guys had a fat wart on his cheek —Don, I think. I kept wanting to stick it with a pin to see what came out. The beer was bad, though, and bad beer's good beer when you're playing cards. Makes you feel like more of a man, I guess. I needed to feel masculine that night.

It wasn't too long after Poker Night One-and-Only that I decided it was time to bail. The city was eating at me. The media wasn't all over me anymore, but there were reminders everywhere. For Christ's sake, I don't know how I stayed there so long, being that my wife was killed across the street. A lot of alcohol, I guess. I also felt obligated for a while, like Jill would have wanted me to stay. Then I realized that was just a bunch of horse shit people say when they're despondent.

Jill had been out planting flowers, of all things. At least I think that's what she was doing. My mind is hazy, and now that I think of it, autumn isn't a planting season. I don't think it is, anyway. Fuck. Regardless, she was out doing some kind of planting/weeding/ digging thing when she was murdered. It wasn't even on our property. She was prettying up the curb area across the street. Town property. That's the kind of person Jill was.

I was sick that week, and was watching game

shows when she was killed. Fucking game shows. That little fact gave me quite the guilt complex later on. But I didn't do anything wrong, damn it. I realize that now. Just because I didn't happen to be outside at the time doesn't mean I did anything wrong. Time of death was set at 6:30 p.m., give or take. I fell asleep around 8:00, and didn't wake up until midnight. I was concerned when I didn't see Jill by my side, so I threw on my jacket over my pajamas.

My Jill lay there for five and a half hours in the rain, body exposed to the world. It took me a half-hour after finding her to compose myself enough to call the police. Detective Morris and I actually had our first chat while I was in my pajamas. I'm sure he gets that all the time though. Cops and priests, I guess, have the most entertaining stories.

Priests can't share their tales of course; that's got to be a bitch. No, I take it back. They *must* tell other priests. No one could resist that kind of temptation, I'm sure of it. No one could resist a good laugh, even at the expense of someone else. *Especially* at the expense of someone else. They probably trade stories like some people trade baseball cards.

When I proposed to Jill, there were no nerves. I felt completely at ease, which some people might say is a bad omen. "No fear, no future"—that's what I've heard. But Jill and I were right for each other, and marriage was only an afterthought. I gave her a ring. She made me take it back, almost angry at the fact that I had given her it. Jill wasn't into pretense or love-proving or hokey traditions.

We spent the money from the ring on our honeymoon—a hokey tradition, for sure, but a damn fine one. I wouldn't have thought there was a woman in this world who would turn down a diamond ring, but I found living proof that I was mistaken. We ended up buying her a faux-silver serpent ring which she wore in a sarcastic fashion, poking fun at normalcy. There's no fun in normalcy.

I remember a guy at work once telling me he fell in love with his wife because she was sane and had good moral values, whatever that means. Those things make for a good coworker, but should be assumed in a life partner. You don't marry someone simply because they're not evil fucks. And maybe your spouse should be a little crazy. Just a little though.

My coworker—the one with the moral wife—was a real animal. I mean a total slob. He left a trail of dirt behind him at all times. It was like he'd never evolved. Probably had himself an os bone. You know what that is? It's a penis bone, and apparently all the other mammals or primates or some crap have 'em. People argue why we lost the damn things, but I figure it's all a conspiracy by those erection people in the lab coats. Couldn't be selling their little pills if we were all walking around with bones in our dicks. I need a bone like that. Some days, anyway. More now than then.

I moved three states south. The particulars aren't important; I just wanted to go warmer. Here's the kicker. When I went, I really went. I needed a new start, so I put my house on the market, and before it even closed I rooted through all my stuff, threw out anything that wasn't completely essential, and packed my car. I told myself if it didn't fit in the car, it wasn't going.

I pulled into a new town with a packed car and a fat wallet. I had taken out a substantial amount of money so that I wouldn't have to fool with the bank for a while. As a life rule, I avoid banks as much as humanly possible. They are soulless institutions. I cheer when they get robbed. And why not? My money's insured. I've always wanted to rob a bank before I die. To shove one of those little notes into some mousy teller's face and scare the shit out of her. I'd love to feel that kind of power just once. Hell, I'd give the money back. Who needs money when you can make people shit their pants?

The first thing I did in my new town of Clefton was go to the park. Not a bad gauge of a place. The cleanliness of the parks is a reflection on a city's integrity. I'd swear by it. The only thing about parks, though, is you have to keep an eye out for the pedophiles and flashers. Parks are like their second home. It's all the kiddies there, I suppose. It's like raw meat to them.

I was quick to get an apartment. Those southern apartments go for the cheap and easy. I bought a bumper sticker. I'll spare you its witticism; suffice to say it was dirty-minded. I'm not the kind of person who would display such a thing on his car, but it sure looked good on my footlocker. I unpacked, and got the bachelor pad into decent shape within hours.

Then I slept the good sleep. It's my hope that death is like sleep. Best eight hours you'll ever spend on this planet, and you get to do it every night.

Ten hours if you pop a pill.

Ten wonderful hours.

Ten.

Hours.

Pills are extraordinary things, and insomnia is Satan's greatest weapon. You know what Satan is? Eat a thick steak. Shit it out, and then eat *that*. Shit again. That's Satan. That's pure evil.

Chapter Four

I often find myself looking at my teeth in the mirror. I look at other people's teeth too. If you use your fingers to spread your lips wide, you can actually see the form of the lower part of your skull. It reminds me of my primality. I think that's why we shit. It keeps us humble. You can't be all that powerful if you still shit.

Jill had beautiful teeth. She lost one in her struggle with Jeff Simons. I don't know if it was ever replaced with a fake by the mortician. The cops told me it would be taken care of, but maybe they lied to comfort me. Cops do that, you know. They say things like, "Oh, he died quickly and bravely," even if he cried like a baby. Or they say, "Finest man I ever served with, ma'am, honest to God."

I guess I would say those things too. I mean, what else can you say? Anyway, Jill was close-mouthed at the wake, of course. I have to laugh when I think of Jill in the afterlife looking like a hockey player. She would have laughed, too, so I don't feel badly about it.

Jill loved rock music. We used to dance naked or semi-naked in our room on Sunday mornings. Neither of us drank coffee, and frankly the newspaper is too depressing for me. So rather than engage in the Sunday tradition that plays out in countless homes across America each week, we'd romp around in our skivvies or thereabouts and jump on the bed to the thrashing of electric guitars. It's hard to believe, I know. Jill often said one of the reasons she fell in love with me was that I am childlike without being childish. We played a lot of games and had a lot of picnics, and that to me is about as close as you can get to the meaning of life.

I think life is actually like a peanut butter and jelly sandwich. It's all about balance. Too much P.B. and your mouth gets all dry. Too much J. and your sandwich gets soggy and drips. Nobody likes a drippy sandwich. I used to call Jill my little J. and she always thought it stood for "Jill." I never told her otherwise. Sometimes you like to keep a little something to yourself.

We used to eat peanut butter and jelly sandwiches by the lake. Another reason Jill and I worked so well together was the fact that we both were intense nature lovers. I once saw her break into tears while staring at a photograph of a wheat field on a calendar at the mall. I kid you not. A fucking wheat field. We took a vacation to the Rockies not long after that. I think she needed it. I think I did too.

My apartment was terrific. It had plenty of windows, a couple of plants left behind by the preceding tenant, and it backed up to a hillside. I had a balcony too. Not much of a view, but a balcony nonetheless. A total steal. I began to wonder why we hadn't lived down here from the start, and then I remembered that back then I needed to get a paycheck in a hurry, and northern cities are good for that. That and little else— angry, clock-run hellholes that they are. There was a little wear and tear to the bathroom, but nothing a little caulking couldn't fix.

When looking for my first real job, I got lucky. A woman named Nancy Trevino interviewed me. I thought it odd at the time being hired by a woman. This was quite a few years ago, remember. Long before the glass ceiling was unceremoniously shattered, though many of the bitchy radicals will tell you it's still there. They won't be happy until we all castrate ourselves or grow breasts or some shit like that. Who knows with those people.

Nancy wore a bun in her hair with one of those sticks in it. I don't know the name; they look a lot like knitting needles. Maybe they're just called hair sticks. Regardless, they look pretty silly. Women wear some peculiar objects: leg warmers, pantyhose, girdles. Who'd want to deal with all that crap? Not to mention "women's issues." Give me a tuxedo and a pair of sweatpants, and I'm good for ten years—double that time if the waistbands are elastic. Women deal with a lot of other funny things, like waxing, 'jama parties, liposuction and being asked out. Silly creatures. There's no sense to be found in any of 'em.

Nancy must have liked something about me, because I got the job. I was fresh out of college with a degree in English, and I had prepared some items to bring to the interview, which would showcase my creativity. I never expected it to work, and I had taken the interview mostly to polish my skills in such situations. I have a tendency to stutter under pressure. Either that or my mouth goes dry. Ever smoke a pack of cigarettes in three hours? Then, you know the feeling.

Anyway, either they were desperate or I came across very well—possibly both—because I started work at Harmon, Inc. the next week. I wasn't given many talents in this world, but I can sure write copy. I worked myself up into a damned good position with my former company, and made a good deal of money in the process. That's probably the one thing I'm really proud about concerning my life. Not the money, but the work. I produced some very good work. I was the guy who came up with "Phisher's Toys are Phantastically Phun." It may sound simple, but it made Mr. Phisher a phortune. And it sticks in your head.

Granted, most of the time I used as my incentive the fact that my writing would pull the wool over the eyes of thousands if not millions of naive, unthinking fucks. But hey, that's the business. And nobody's forcing you to buy a thirty-dollar pair of underwear just 'cause the women in the commercials tell you they prefer them. These are the same women who mocked you in grade school and dated guys named Brad.

I've done things that I'm ashamed of. We all have, no? I once called my mother a bitch. I stole a basketball I had the money to pay for, just to see if I could get away for it. The clerk must have thought I was one damn ugly pregnant woman, or maybe he just didn't care that I was stealing. Saved him the trouble of ringing it up. I didn't even play basketball. What was I thinking?

I tried coke twice. Try it once, and you can say you were experimenting. Try it twice and well, whatever. I'm no moralist. Worst thing I ever did? Probably hitting a woman in the elevator in the Riggs building. She was being a real bitch, and it had been a tough day. It wasn't openhanded. It was a flat-out punch. I ran out of the elevator to escape any would-be big-ass boyfriend that might be waiting. I told you, I'm ashamed of it. So I cursed my mother and left-hooked a nasty bitch. Not very nice things, for sure, but I don't deserve to be a widower so young.

You tell me there's a God, and I tell you there's a big, orange unicorn that lives in the Pacific Ocean and hands out laxatives. A force? Maybe. A kind and loving God? Shit, I more believe Santa Claus is gonna glide down my chimney this winter. Not after what happened to Jill. Maybe that unicorn can give one of his laxatives to Jeffrey Simons.

Oh, one more thing about my friend the Solemn Stalker. Seems his morally decent life has one ink-spot. Apparently, the folks living in his neighborhood when he was a youth remember him throwing stones at squirrels, pulling on cats' tails till they scratched and bit (the cats, not their tails), picking at road kill with sticks, that kind of thing. His parents denied it, but of course, they're biased. One reporter referred to it as a blemish on an otherwise impeccable record. A "blemish"? You get your rocks off hurting defenseless animals, they should put you away for life. You think that might be just a small sign that the light's burning a little dim in the attic? That the meter needs feeding? I almost fell off my chair when I heard about Mr. Simon's boyhood hobby for the first time. His neighbors should have shot him on-sight right then and there. I'd still have my little J. if they had. Fuck you, Jeff. I hope the food sucks where you are.

Chapter Five

They're funny, the things that happen in this life. I met Cristen Powers in the deli while picking up lunchmeat for my new apartment. Like I said earlier, I don't normally go up to strange women and chat them up. Thing is, I knew I'd never love again so why even bother trying? I'd never match what I had had, and all trying could bring was heartache. Nothing and nobody could ever fill the void left when that bastard raped and slaughtered my entire world. Knowing this, rejection didn't matter. What did I care what this pip-squeak, black-haired woman thought of me? Besides, I wasn't looking for a date; I just felt like commenting on her backpack accessorizing.

"Great patch. Have you ever seen them?"

"Them" referred to The Velvet Delusion, a band that Jill and I had seen a few times up north. Frankly, I was surprised that they were big enough to be known way the hell down here. Ms. Black-Hair had a black and yellow patch sewn onto her pack. The letters V.D. were scripted on a background strewn with question marks lying in different positions. To someone unfamiliar with the band, the patch might have raised questions, but I saw them play before I saw their logo. I have a feeling the band's initials are more than coincidence. It's hard to forget V.D., and it made for good word-of-mouth advertising.

"Oh, yeah, many times. I usually go up to Binter to catch them at the Sin Bin." The woman was pleasant and smelled of honey. She spoke in a mother's tone—soothing and mellow.

"I was actually kind of surprised to see your patch. I didn't think they'd know V.D. down here." People turned and looked at me. I lowered my voice. "I'm from Drexton—their hometown."

"No kidding. I used to wait tables up there when I was younger. Well, outside of Drexton, anyway. Lafarre."

Lafarre was 45 minutes from Drexton, which I supposed technically counts as outside. The woman adjusted her pack, lifting it higher on her back, and turned to face me. I was feeling very comfortable speaking with her, and I was hoping the line in front of us would take its time of it.

We spoke for about ten minutes, until she was waited on by a man in green pants. She ordered three pounds of bologna. I remember thinking, *What in the hell does someone do with three pounds of bologna?*

After she was waited on, she turned back to continue our conversation. That's always a sign that the conversation is going well. Anybody can kill time waiting for bologna or a bank deposit or even a haircut, but to continue talking afterward says, "You're more interesting than whatever I'm doing next," even if that's just putting away bologna. We talked for another half-hour, and like I said, her name is Cristen Powers. I was glad it wasn't a "J" name. I think I'm retiring that letter.

It's a good thing I didn't know at the time how she spells her name. I would have figured the alternative 'C' to mean "new-age, hippie parents" which means one of two things: new-age, hippy daughter or tight-assed bitch. People always either conform or rebel. There's no middle ground, I'm sure. Either way, I would never have had continued relations with Cristen. I guess that goes to show something, but the hell if I know what. I don't need your patronizing tone—not today, you arrogant son of a bitch. I know you're thinking of Samantha, out there by that tree, but she is for later.

Cristen informed me that Velvet Delusion was playing in two months in Binter City. She was going with two friends, and told me I should get a ticket so we could all tailgate. She took my number (*she* took *my* number; boy, times had changed) and told me she'd call when the evening of the concert drew nearer.

I was strangely disappointed that I had to wait two months to see Cristen again. No matter; we were just going to be friends. You had better believe I bought a ticket that very same day. I'd never heard of The Sin Bin, of course, but it must have been fairly large and well-known, 'cause they took credit card orders by phone. That's unusual for concerts, right? Normally they make you pay at the door. Maybe I'm just getting old.

Jill was barren. I think that's the word for it. Anyway, she couldn't have children. *We* couldn't have children. No, *she* couldn't have children. Facts are facts. Some kind of egg implantation failure. Not enough stick in her uterus, I guess. I think she felt guilty about it to a degree, but it didn't bother me a bit. I was never gung-ho on the idea of kids, though I wouldn't go so far as to say that could we have had children, I'd be having them just for her sake. Suffice it to say, kids weren't a priority for me. I wanted kids like some people want a dog, which probably means it was a good thing she couldn't have them. I mean, shit in a diaper or on the rug, is there really that much difference?

I often think of where I'd be now if Jill and I had procreated. Up a certain creek, that's where. I could barely take care of *myself* at the time of Jill's untimely passing, let alone children. In retrospect, it's probably good that she had the little uterus that couldn't. The only thing I feel bad about is the amount of emotional pain it caused Jill. She really wanted children. I think the woman was just so full of love that she needed more outlets for it.

Her last name had been McIntyre. Pretty name, isn't it? Jill McIntyre. Sounds like a woman who lives up in the hills and hands out shiny, red apples to neighborhood children. "Where are you going, Master William?" "Oh, Mamá, I'm just going to old lady McIntyre's to get a crisp." Whoever started calling children "Master" this and that, needs to come back to life and get hit by a train.

Jill Caine isn't so bad either. "Ed and Jill Caine on a stroll down Lovers' Lane," we used to say. Well, she used to say it. It's a bit corny for a man's tastes. Jill called me Edward; I liked that she did. I once called her Jillian. She didn't take to that so much. I never called her Jillian again, even during our very rare arguments.

She had two brothers. The younger of the two was named Iggy. Not short for Ignatious or anything punk like that. Just Iggy. He works as a laborer for a contracting company and speaks with an inexplicable light British accent. Damnedest thing you'd ever hear, and it comes on strong when he's been imbibing. Not in the way that some people affect an accent to appear blue-blooded. This is real.

Iggy and I got on well. He was and is a simple man living a simple life. The man has a sink full of friends. He doesn't take himself too seriously and is as funny as the day is long. He's good people. I haven't seen him since the funeral. My fault, not his.

Jill's other brother is named Charles. I never met Charles. He was born with a mental blip, as I once heard it euphemized. He was "the other McIntyre." He's resided at Dayton Institution since he was quite young. He earned his room and board by burning down a public building, after which they were forced to retain him for, um, a while. People tend to get upset when you burn down their buildings, especially when people work inside of them. The employees did manage to get out in time, but Charles had used a decent accelerant, and the firefighters were a little tardy in their arrival. Apparently there wasn't much left of the place in the end. Knowing now what I didn't know then, I often wonder his intent in setting the fire. Maybe he was too smart for his own good.

Jill didn't see Charles after she was ten, which must have meant he was pretty far into the next world. I once overheard Jill's dad talking to a friend about his elder son while having drinks. It seems his brain was deteriorating, and after a few months of being institutionalized, he qualified as human only in the barest terms. All rationality was gone, like with those children raised by wolves. I don't know why nature is so cruel, but it sure makes the world more interesting.

To think of it, Jill had a pretty tough life. Between losing Charles to insanity or whatever you want to call it and losing her mother to a car accident, she had endured her share of pain and then some. This makes the fact that she was such a bright-shining person all the more remarkable. I like to think I had something to do with it, though I probably did not. I can only hope that her death was not too painful. She deserved a quiet exit. I had hoped she would go as a silver-haired princess smiling in her sleep.

My apartment was looking dandy. I had stuck with the minimalist mentality, and my living room had only a rug, a television, and two beanbag chairs. Nice ones, though, not the kind where the beads fall out and make a mess. Those are for college kids who need a place to get lucky without fear of rug burn.

I would open the sliding glass door, and my apartment would suddenly feel like a cabana. I got the afternoon sunshine, which to me is the best two-word phrase in the English language next to Happy Hour. My new oval rug was rather interesting too. It was black, with a zigzag of yellow tracing its edges, looking not unlike lightning bolts in the nighttime sky. The rug was soft and sweet on the ass. There are two things you should never skimp on in this world: carpeting and toilet paper. Your feet and ass deserve better, really they do.

Two months came and went like a shot. I was taking to my new town and was able to get through the day without once getting weepy. I now thought of Jill as being by my side, guiding me. Now, don't get me wrong. I'm no spiritualist or séance-holding sage, and I wasn't seeing ghosts. It's just more comforting to think of someone you love in a good situation than to think of them as rotting underground. It wasn't like I thought she was some sort of guardian angel or any of that horse shit. I'm aware that she's fertilizer by now.

Jill wasn't cremated. That was one thing we disagreed on. To her, the idea of the cemetery was a romantic one, which might sound odd. I guess she liked the idea of being buried with your loved ones and having the sun shine upon you. Maybe I'll have myself buried just to make her happy. Maybe not. Something about bugs in my brain and maggots in my testicles.

For my money, cemeteries are the biggest and most selfish waste of space since golf courses. Or vice versa. I guess people have been dying longer than they've been golfing. Every time someone bogies, they should be shot on site and buried where they stand. We could kill two birds with one gravestone.

As it turned out, it was an hour's drive to Binter. I followed Cristen and her friends in my car while they rode in her pickup. They offered me what would no doubt have been a very crowded ride, but I politely declined. These people were new to me, and I wanted to be able to scram in a hurry if I wasn't having fun. Also, it's nice to be able to stretch out in your own car. My car wasn't big, and I couldn't really stretch out all that much, but it still made me feel better to ride alone. I think it's good to do things on your own—sink or swim—even if it just means driving separately once in a while. Otherwise you get weak.

We stopped at a drive-thru beer joint to get a couple of cases. They paid. I made a mental note to buy them something at the concert in return for their kindness. *Only to the kind doth kindness come.* I read that somewhere as a kid. Whoever wrote it needs a strong enema, I'm sure.

There was a cooler in the bed of the truck filled with hot dogs and snacks. Cristen's friend Pat had brought along his charcoal grill to cook on. I wanted some mellow music for the ride, so I popped in a classical composer. One of the B's, I think. I enjoy all types of music, but I am knowledgeable about very little of it. I like to let the magician keep his dirty little secrets to himself.

I was surprised by the size of Binter City. It's a legitimate "city," though it doesn't get much press. It must be a sleepy town. We pulled onto Third Avenue and into the parking lot of the Sin Bin. I remember thinking it odd that we'd tailgate at a club. Normally I associate it with an arena-complex atmosphere. And normally it's just a bunch of young hooligans, not a mixed group like the one at the Bin that day. What's tailgating without painted faces and a couple of water bongs?

I dropped my preconceived ideas when I saw the number of people out back drinking beer and cooking up dinner. What a waste of skin this all was. A bunch of slobbering drunks, slaves to the beast within.

The Sin Bin had a huge parking lot, though the

club itself didn't look all that sizable, contrary to my earlier assumption. I didn't know how all of the people before me would ever fit through the front door.

My observation of the parking lot is the last thing I recall from that night.

Chapter Six

It was 9:30 am, and I smelled eggs. My stomach felt uneasy, and I moved slowly so as not to upset it further. The eggy smell certainly didn't help, though it did make my stomach growl. I worked my way into a crawling position and peeked over the half-wall next to the sofa I was laid out on. I had no idea where I was.

Cristen tended to the stove, listening to music over headphones. I suddenly got a whiff of an odor far worse than that of the eggs. I looked to my right, too quickly. My stomach whined in complaint. There was a brown bag there that reeked of vomit. It was a wet, brown smell. The picture was starting to become clear. I opened my mouth to speak, but found my lips and tongue were dried out. My head didn't feel particularly good either, so I decided the situation was safe, and an explanation could wait. I put my head down on the pillow, and slept for two more hours. It wasn't great sleep, but it helped.

"Ed..."

"Ed..."

"Edward..."

Vague recognition. I opened my eyes to see two aspirin on the table in front of me, along with a towering blue glass of water. It might as well have been solid gold at that point. I reached for the glass. She had over poured, and the outside of the glass was wet with droplets. The cool water felt good against my hand.

"I thought you might appreciate that."

I turned my head to see Cristen. She wasn't wearing the robe I saw her in earlier by the stove. She had showered and put her hair up, and she was now in a green shirt. The bottom was oranged by bleach and torn with age. I wondered how many men that shirt had known more intimately than me. Jill had men before Ed Caine, of course. I thought of them all in bed with her, naked. And all the women they had been with collectively. It would have had to have been a pretty big bed. It was a thought I wished to put out of my head immediately. I rubbed my eyes because they were still weak and cloudy. At last I gathered myself and spoke.

"I do appreciate it. Thank you."

"No problem. Would you like something to eat?" I was starving, but I didn't care to impose anymore than I had obviously done already.

"No, thank you. I take it this is your apartment?"

"Yep. We're back in Clefton. I think you overdid it a bit last night."

"I haven't had a drink in six months. Kind of a promise I made to myself. Last night was the first time since then that I felt comfortable taking a sip." Technically a lie. I had broken down two months ago and had a light beer. That doesn't count though. Light beer is a ball game in a domed stadium.

"You must have felt damn comfortable." She said it in a kidding, sprite-like way. She had a very pleasant voice. A mother has that voice—I'll say it again. Like on the mornings when you wake up sick and can't go to school and they serve you warm gelatin. Yeah, a mother has just that kind of voice.

"How much did I drink?"

"Between the lot and the club, probably fifteen. I wasn't keeping count though. I'm not your mother."

"I haven't blacked out like this since I was a kid. I'm really sorry."

She tossed me a smile and took a seat on the chair beside the sofa.

"Hey, no problem. You were really hamming it up last night, dancing with all kinds of people."

"I don't dance. My wife, um...my ex....Jill used to kid me all the time about it. It's not in my blood."

"Well, whatever. But you did dance. You had the whole place in stitches." She paused, apparently aware that it was taking me a second to register. "How'd you like V.D.?"

"Unfortunately, I don't remember seeing them."

"Well, I'm sorry you don't. My friends loved you though. Sandy thought you were witty. Quite the shit." Sandy was tall and straight-bodied with muscular extremities. I remembered wondering if she played volleyball. Her forearms were bread loaves.

"How'd I get back?"

"We gave you a ride, though we had to leave your car there. I didn't want to go fishing for your keys, you understand. They don't tow since they close so late. I'll take you to get it when you're feeling up to it."

I had stopped listening. I was captivated by the small nubs poking at the front of her shirt. As a boy, we're taught to like them big, but we come to find that the little perky ones are actually the best. They seem to smile at you. I was staring pretty good, too.

I wondered if Cristen sensed it. I wondered if maybe she was puffing her chest out a little in response. The games we play, they're so funny. Wrapping ourselves in polyester and suede, as if the parts beneath stop swingin' and sweatin' when we get on the subway or walk into the office. These days, all you have to do is remind a woman that she *is* a woman and you'll elicit a smile. It makes them feel good to see that someone noticed. That's how I got Alisha—the freak.

Ah, the three women in my life. The Angel, the Freak, and the Slut. Cristen was a slut; I could sense it. It sounds like some kind of twisted fairy tale or really bad joke. An angel, a freak, and a slut are in a bar talking about their best sex. The freak tells about a time in a bondage bar. The slut relates a story of once having had six men at once. The angel tells the others about an encounter on Cloud Nine. So the freak chimes in. "Sex on a cloud. Sounds dangerous. How do you do it?" To which the angel replies, "Ah, you just wing it."

I warned you it was bad, now, didn't I?

Cristen rose from her seat and walked toward the refrigerator. She poured orange juice into one of the big, blue glasses. I really did admire those glasses. I snapped back to reality. Her tits weren't going anywhere.

"Look, I really appreciate all this. You could have just left me there. A lot of people would have."

"It's no problem, Ed. We all got to look out for each other, no?" She gave me a wink that left me unexpectedly excited.

The morning progressed into afternoon, and I took a shower, for which I was grateful beyond belief. The nozzle was high, and the water was hot and jetted with good pressure. The three keys to a good shower and thus a better life: heat, height, and pressure.

We jumped in the pickup to go get my car. Normally, hangovers don't go away fully until after your second night of sleep. For some reason, your body needs to go through two full sleep cycles to right itself. That day, though, I felt better. It must have been the company, though the shower helped, too.

We talked at the start of the ride. It was very comfortable, and we found we had similar tastes in quite a few areas. Cristen was very spunky, as reflected in her look. She had spiky hair and wore a tight, red shirt. While Jill had been tall and slender, Cristen was shorter with an athletic build. What little hair she sported was a brilliant black, and she had sun-freckles on her cheeks that made her look cherubic. She was a very cute woman. I hadn't noticed before.

"Ed, do you mind if I ask you a question? It's a bit personal."

"Sure."

"You mentioned that you were married. How long have you been divorced?" I liked Cristen, but I didn't feel comfortable with this topic yet. I skirted it.

"Eighteen months."

"You know you didn't pass out right away, right?"

"What do you mean?" I hate quick transitions. This seemed a strange diversion from the divorce question.

"Last night, at the club. Seems you made a friend." She winked at me. I think she expected a question from me at this point, because she sure took her time in chiming in again.

"You don't remember?"

"No."

"I think his name was Frank. The house painter?"

"Shit, I don't remember him at all."

"I'd have thought you would. You two got along pretty well, I'd say. I mean, he *did* steal a kiss from you."

I looked Cristen dead in the eye, or as near as I could while she was driving. The cab was silent. Now, I have nothing against gays (less competition for chicks, in my mind), but I know what I am, and it's not gay. I wanted to just say "Bullshit" and end it there. But there's always that small part of you...alcohol does some strange shit to your head. I felt little bugs on my skin. I tried to remember the guy—any guy—from last night. Finally, Cristen laughed loudly.

"Ha! You had to think about it, huh?"

I laughed along, but the incident bothered me for a while. Why did I hesitate? What would my delay cause Cristen to believe? I had wondered about her own sexuality. Was this her way of bringing it to light? Of testing the waters? I was driving myself crazy in her truck. People say we're all on this big continuum and that there is no man and woman or straight and gay. Fuck. I hate gray areas. It reminds me of that pin: "Bisexuals are greedy fuckers." It always makes me laugh.

I sat there in silence for a while. I'm not sure why, but Cristen did too. I knew I'd still like her if she was gay, but I also knew I felt uncomfortable at the thought she might think *I* was. It's a fucked-up world. I'm telling you, the millennium brought with it a warm wind carrying death on its shoulders. The world just ain't the same anymore.

Six months went by. I adapted to my new town and took a job editing for a local paper. It paid lousy, but I wasn't out for money at that point. I needed something to keep me busy. When I interviewed, the man who was asking the questions recognized my name. He began to question me about the murder and then halted himself mid-sentence, embarrassed and ashamed. In the end, I think he took pity on me. It was either pity or guilt. I got the job though, so it didn't bother me a stitch. Pity's underrated; it can get you a drink, a smoke, a lay. Nothing wrong with that. No, sir, not a damn thing wrong with that.

Cristen talked me into joining a group that picks litter up off the roads with one of those stabby apparatuses. The guys in the park use them too.

Personally I think it's a cool job, cleaning up the outdoors in the comfort of green overalls. You have to respect the people who do it for a living. Altruism is rare, and rewarding only to those with the largest and purest of hearts.

It made me feel good to be outside in the open air, helping the community and all that crap. It amazed me how many people would throw trash out their window—cigarette butts, tissues—even as they passed us while we were working. It was an endless cycle. People are pigs without the good looks and the brains.

Eventually I did tell Cristen about Jill.

It was a rainy night. We had become pretty good friends by then, considering the relatively short length of our relationship. We were in my apartment after a day working the roads. We sipped wine on the balcony, which is covered by an overhang. I purchased some plastic green chairs down at Arnie's Home and Garden, and they were practical if not stylish. I tried hanging a dart board on the wall dividing my balcony from the next, but I found that was just a convenient way to lose darts over the railing. Also, my neighbors below cook out a lot. I didn't want a stray dart to peg their kid in the eye, and have to spend the evening searching for his cornea in the grass.

We were sipping zinfandel—not my favorite wine type, but Cristen liked it, so it was fine by me. Personally, I don't think wine should come in shades. It should be RED or WHITE. There's too much wishy-washiness in the world today. Paper or plastic. Cash or credit. Buy or lease. Make a decision and live with it, for crying out loud.

We were relaxing, shooting the breeze, but my mind wasn't in it. I kept looking off in the distance, daydreaming, and Cristen must have noticed it. I broke off mid-sentence and began to cry.

"What's wrong, Edward?" What's wrong? What's wrong?

It's a question we all have heard about a billion times, not that anyone ever solves any of our problems. I am only comforted by the fact that should people stop fucking here and now for the next sixty years, this miserable experience would all be over with. But who's gonna convince the people to stop fucking? It's like the cat and the mice and the bell.

So I told her about Jill. I told her all that I've told you, Doctor. It was a long and emotional conversation. She was very receptive and listened far more than she talked, and that's a very good and rare quality in a friend. Yes, she was a very good crisis listener. The conversation ended in a hug, and I remember how that felt. Her body was warm, soft. It wasn't one of those obligatory hugs with quick shoulder pats and a stiff frame. You know, man hugs. It was heartfelt.

The rain changed direction and was now swooping in on us, but I didn't care. I don't think Cristen did either. The rain felt good, natural, primal. She kissed me. So much for my thoughts about her sexual orientation. This would be a hell of a "favor." Her lips were soft. Some women don't have soft lips. Some have lifeless, rough lips. Lifeless, rough lips are a sign of a woman without depth and are to be avoided.

She pulled back from the kiss, ashamed. After the conversation we had just completed, I think she felt like she was taking advantage of a vulnerable man. I pulled her back in and kissed her back. It felt good. No, it felt great. Not great like they do in college, when it's exciting and new. This kiss was deep, passionate, caring. Jill and I had shared many such kisses. What surprised me though was that it wasn't just reassuring. Out there on the balcony, in the rain, it felt right and wonderful.

We walked inside, and she spent the night. I'd have to say that was one of the top five nights of my life, and not because of the sex (or at least not exclusively). That night, for the first time in over two years, I felt human. I felt alive. I hoped that somewhere, somehow, Jill saw me that night and nodded her approval. I think she would have liked Cristen. No, I'm sure she would have.

The next morning I awoke—always a good thing, and I suppose Cristen figured turnabout to be fair play, because she took it upon herself to open up. I know that I can repeat this now, though at the time I swore myself mum.

Cristen had been in a long and serious relationship beginning when she was fifteen. It was your typical rebellion affair at the start; basically Jimmy was the perfect type to piss off the parents and bring a little bit of an independent feeling into a young girl's life.

Eventually though, her motives changed, as she found herself falling in love with the tall, charming James Youngblood. James was eighteen when they'd met at a diner. Cristen had been having a cheeseburger with her friends when he approached her. Well, she took to his charismatic style, and they began to date. When she turned eighteen, she moved in with Jimmy, against the wishes of her parents. The decision created a rift between Cristen and her folks that wasn't mended until she was twenty-five. At that time her father fell ill (he has since recovered). Cristen returned home to help care for him, and she and her parents decided that enough water had passed under the bridge and that it was time to put an end to it.

Anyway, Cristen moved in with Jimmy. He had a one-bedroom apartment and drove a truck intrastate. He was gone long hours, which gave Cristen time to see her friends and take a job of her own. She was still very young, and was not ready at the time to commit most of her time to one person, although she did love Jimmy dearly. Four months after moving into the apartment, she became pregnant. Between the two of them, Cristen and Jimmy actually made enough money to live a decent lifestyle (Cristen had taken her first landscaping job). Two jobs, two mouths is an entirely different equation than one job, three mouths, however. Together, the couple decided that the timing wasn't right. Frankly, they were young and scared.

Cristen made an appointment, and two weeks later, well, the baby was nothing more than a moot point and a stain on the operating table. It was at that point that the couple started using birth control. In retrospect, Cristen admitted that they were quite lucky to have avoided pregnancy for as long as they did.

Well, they wouldn't be so lucky again. Within three months, Cristen found herself pregnant for the second time. Now nineteen, she was distraught. The first time hadn't been so bad actually, but now guilt was beginning to eat at her, as she now felt like murder—I mean abortion—was becoming a form of contraception rather than damage control, if you will. She fought with herself this time over what to do, and the biggest problem was that she found Jimmy to be very unsupportive on the issue.

Cristen wished to have the baby, essentially saying damn the consequences. She didn't think she could excuse herself two abortions, and she also didn't want to put her own body through that strain a second time. She didn't know, too, if the doctors would perform the procedure so soon after the first occurrence, and she was afraid to ask. When Cristen was telling me this, I couldn't help but think about how very badly Jill had wanted to get pregnant. Now, my logical side realizes circumstances were different for the two women, but the first thought through my mind was one woman's treasure is another woman's trash.

The normally reasonable James Youngblood didn't like the idea of his future being decided when he was twenty-two, and insisted Cristen not have the baby. In the end, fear and simple economics won out over heartfelt emotion and Cristen made another appointment. She found, though, that she could no longer face Jimmy. Two weeks after her second abortion, Cristen broke up with her longtime boyfriend and moved out. She had to work longer and harder hours now, but she felt it was something that had to be done. She feared now that, as a result of the abortions, perhaps she would never be able to bear children when she was ready. Quietly I hoped—just for a second—that this was true. There's nothing like a good backup form of birth control.

I dismissed that thought immediately, don't get me wrong. I realized it was a dreadful, awful, horrible thought, but after all that had happened in my life those past few years, I might as well be honest. It truly is the best policy. We can't control these little thoughts that creep into the recesses of our mind. The human brain is a sublime piece of machinery, but it can also be one hell of a monstrosity. Consider the items it has come up with in the past: cannibalism, necrophilia, mustard gas, the guillotine, quartering, disco.

We don't like to admit these little invasive ideas to ourselves. We try to drown them out. But the taboo and the dangerous thought is a driving force in society, and secretly we all get off a little bit on the thoughts we shouldn't be having. They are our dirty little secrets, something just for us.

Now it was Cristen's turn to cry, and my turn to provide the soft shoulder on which to do so. I remember even now that at one point her cheek rubbed up against my arm, brushing tears onto my bicep. There was a window directly behind the bed, and as the sun shone in, the tears glistened upon my arm. I experienced a great happiness at that moment. It was a happiness to be alive.

Here we were, two people crying about our problems, and yet I was thrilled to be alive. Seeing those tears reminded me that, much as we like to hide it, we are all still human. There is a world of opportunity before us. We're creating our own movie with our own plot twists, and the ending is largely under our control... well, all except the final curtain.

That morning, in that bed, I felt vibrant and passionate, and unstoppable. I wanted to play first base for a professional ballclub, and I didn't even care for sports. I settled for gin rummy. It was Cristen's favorite. I'm glad I played her game. If I had known she'd be dead so soon afterwards, I would have let her win.

I prefer spades myself. It requires just the right amount of thinking. Bridge is a better game, but it's dying because it requires too long an attention span for the modern world of microwaves and text messaging. Other games such as Crazy 8s are too simplistic. Spades is a good in-betweener. You could spend your whole lifetime playing it and still be learning when you die. But rummy is a good talking game. It doesn't require much effort or concentration, and it has a nice pace to it. I got lucky on the first hand; I drew three fives.

"Isn't it funny how you can't *not* think?" Cristen

studied her cards as she asked the question.

"Come again?" I was hoping the five of diamonds was near the top of the pile. I like to get off to a fast start.

"Well, it's very difficult to clear your mind. There are complex techniques just for doing so. Your brain is always on, and there's nothing you can do about it. I often wonder, who's in charge, you or your brain?"

I figured Cristen was just humoring me. She knew full well that psychology is a pet topic of mine. I don't study it deeply or technically, but I do like to try to figure out what makes us all tick.

"I guess it's kind of like the idea of, if you theoretically cut out a chunk of brain and then another chunk and another, how far could you go and still call yourself human? I mean, what *is* human? Our brains? Our souls? Our emotions?" Truly, I'd love to know the answer to that.

"And another thing. We don't even control our minds, it would seem. I mean, if I were to suggest an image to you, there's no way you could help but imagine it."

"Try me." I felt up for a challenge from the slut. That was now my pet name for her. Of course, I never said it aloud, but it made me laugh inside. Slut. Slut. Slut. What a funny word.

"Okay. Don't think of a walrus with a lacrosse stick shoved up its butt."

I laughed and tried to think of a big bowl of gelatin. A big bowl of blue gelatin. A big bowl of boiling, blue gelatin. A walrus with a lacrosse stick up its butt. Damn. I just could not get away from the image.

"That's not fair. That's too graphic. I almost *wanted* to picture that because it's so laughable."

"Fair enough. Let's try another."

"You've got the damn five of diamonds, don't you."

"Hush. Don't change the subject. Here's an easy, nondescript one. Don't think of —and had she said "a bowl of blue gelatin," I would have left for Vegas immediately—an orange cup."

Big bowl of gelatin. Big bowl of blue gelatin. Big

bowl of boiling, blue gelatin. Big bowl of boiling, blue, bubbly gelatin. Uh, oh, running out of 'B' words. Big bowl of boiling, blue, bubbly, orange cup. Damn.

"All right, you win." I really wanted to beat her little test, hoping that I was more than just a sheep. Alas, I am not. To top it off, she laid down the two, three, four, and five of diamonds. We were doing more talking than playing, but now I was forced to change my strategy. I hate when that happens. Having to drop the idea of four of a kind, I instead would go after a high straight. I had the jack and king of clubs.

"So I guess you're right. We're too smart for our own damn good. Care to distract me some more?"

"Hey, if you can't talk and play cards at the same time, you've got bigger issues to worry about than rummy. Could you grab the pen behind you? I've got a scratch pad right here." She reached toward my nightstand, and continued talking.

"All right, I got another one. How do blind people know if they're straight or gay if they can't see what people look like?" Obviously she didn't have much faith in her hand if she had to resort to such distraction tactics. I felt confident.

"I don't know. I guess it's kind of internal. Or maybe they go by pheromones."

"Well, if it *is* internal, that would prove that orientation is preprogrammed."

"I think most people assume it's a nature thing anyway. I guess you could argue that the blind take the orientation of their parents, go with what they are taught as a kid. Kind of like, it's easier to go with the flow." I reconsidered a moment. "That doesn't work, though, 'cause it's not always the case. At least I assume it's not always the case. Besides, you're overlooking the fact that it's more than the look. It's the essence and the touch and the mind of the person as well. I sure wouldn't find you all that attractive if you had the mind and the smell and the touch of Joe Ironworker. Male and female is about a lot more than looks."

"I bet they must really enjoy making love— heightened senses and all. I bet you we can't even imagine the level of pleasure their bodies reach, because we're not so in tune with our bodies."

"Never thought of it, and it's about *time* I got the queen."

I laid down the straight. I had already set down three nines. The hand was out.

"All right, Ed. What's that, 55 points?"

"Yeah."

She smiled at me. I smiled back. The world was smiling.

Smile. It's a comforting, warm word.

Smile. Nobody loves you.

The great bologna mystery had been solved the week before. Cristen bought it en masse so she could feed the birds behind her apartment. I argued that it was probably not particularly good for their health, but she retorted that it was probably not particularly good for ours either. I couldn't argue that.

We ended up together till 4:00 p.m.. We both felt very comfortable, and neither of us had anywhere in particular to go, and let's face it, Sundays are the perfect do-nothing day. It's a time for coffee and danish and dozing off. It is a day for rest, so says God. And who the hell am I to question Him? We watched a black-and-white flick on channel 47. It was grainy, simply-plotted, and terribly enjoyable. You have to love movies that don't take themselves too seriously.

You have to love *people* who don't take themselves too seriously.

Chapter Seven

Not much happened that week. I worked. I slept. I ate. Really. Not much.

Chapter Eight

Saturday. I window-shopped at an outdoor mall. In truth, it's a strip mall with a whole bunch of vendors on the sidewalk in addition to the stores. You might have assumed that anyway. The moms and the pops are long dead and buried, and it's a strip mall world. I was really quite enjoying myself, and I even managed to pick myself up a stereo. Well, not a stereo, per se, but one of those boom boxes that were all the rage in the '80s. It was marked down thirty percent and had a 3-CD deck. The guy who sold it to me was a real cutup. He looked like a cartoon character, with his long, blond sideburns, beady little eyes and strong jaw line. He was also an incredibly massive man.

Like many incredibly massive men, he wore an incredibly undersized tee shirt to assure himself that the world would know that he'd put his time in at the gym. As a general rule, I don't like anybody who can bench press me. I suppose it's just jealousy. He wore sneakers, and one of them had a loosened sole that went "Schlup, Schlup" when he walked. It was very annoying. It reminded me of a joke I heard as a kid, something about an elephant and a puddle. Like I said, though, he was a real card. He was also one of those guys who believes the moon landing was an in-studio thing.

I spent a lot more time in that store than I had intended. He kept jawing away, and to his credit he made me laugh quite a bit. I guess the store didn't get much business; he seemed awfully lonely. Finally, I was able to take the receipt from his hand and sneak in a word edgewise. I thanked him for his time, and headed out the door.

I wasn't three steps out the door when an incredibly skinny woman ran me down from the right. I had my head turned and was standing still when she plowed into me. My newly purchased radio fell to the ground, and there was an audible crack. Instinctively, I hit the woman. Now, generally I'm not a woman-hitter other than the bitch I mentioned earlier; bitches don't count. I've never hit a girlfriend, and really, I didn't mean to hit this woman either. It just happened. I was having a good day, it was sunny, all systems go, and then—wham-bam-boom—this woman crashes through me like I didn't exist. Who the hell do these people think they are? They're the same damn people who yell at the bank tellers and hold up the grocery line counting pennies. Frankly, I'm glad I hit the sorry twig. Somebody needed to.

I left the radio where it sat on the ground, assuming it was beyond repair. I was halfway to my car when I decided I wasn't leaving without a radio, so I went in to see Studly Gotmuscle again.

"Problems?" He was wadding up paper and chucking it at the wastebasket. There were a dozen or so misses staggered on the floor.

"I need another radio. Same kind."

"You giving it as a gift? We have gift cards, you know. Certificates too."

"No. No gift. I just need..."

It was then that the door opened with a start. The stick was back with some guy who I can only assume was her boyfriend. He had three inches on me, and about thirty pounds.

"Who the hell do you think you are, hitting a woman?!"

"I didn't hit her." I lied. "She plowed into me and broke my radio. That's why I'm back in here in the first place."

"Are you calling Missy here a liar?" His tone was deadly, and his voice was loud. He had one of those creepy spider-web tattoos on his elbow.

Mr. Workout stepped in from behind the counter.

"Sir, please keep your voice down. You'll upset the other customers." There *were* no other customers in the store at the time, but I wasn't about to point this fact out. I felt it was in my best interest to keep quiet.

"This doesn't concern you, freak."

I can only imagine that in his anger, Mr. X forgot who he was talking to, because my new best friend stood up and approached him.

"Now it does. I told you to quiet down, and I'm not going to ask you again." It was a string of words I had heard time and time again, and it was becoming tiresome. I was hoping they'd get right to the good stuff; I needed a distraction.

Well, fortunately for me, boys will be boys. The boyfriend was now all into it with the clerk. They began trading insults. Apparently his girlfriend's problems took a back seat to his own situation. While they were circling and eyeing each other like cobra and mongoose, I quietly slipped out the door, now feeling quite content to leave radioless.

I guess it's only logical that people act like animals; after all, we *are* animals. But it's especially humorous to see two guys arguing, sizing one another up. Equally funny is when a man and a woman flirt—the equivalent of the goofy courtship dance among some birds, I presume. I guess anger and lust are the only motivations powerful enough to persuade us to drop the facade we call humanity, if only for a few minutes to fight or fuck.

The incident at the storefront got me to thinking. Specifically, I imagined that moment when you are nearing someone who is walking towards you on a sidewalk. Obviously, someone has to move laterally. Now, sometimes you both move, and fall into that left-right-left, am-I-avoiding-you-or-are-you-avoiding-me situation when hopefully you both end up wearing smiles.

Most of the time, though, most of the time it is I who gives way. And I got around to thinking right there or then about why that is. Is it just that I am an extraordinary person, or is there something more to it? Do I come off as a pushover, as submissive even? And if so, how would people sense this without even talking to me? It's not as though I'm undersized or anything like that. My next thought was pheromones, but I was doubtful that they could be picked up on so quickly from a distance, especially on a crowded sidewalk. Still, something's going on here. The future is now, and the rules are all changing.

Technological advancement has changed the world, and not only in the way you're thinking. It's more than just practical. Now even the weakest, the dimmest, the least charismatic can rise to the top, or be bred into the system with a big bank account. Evolution can no longer thin out the crowd, and it's only a matter of time until nature bites back big-time. Think Black Plague. Think AIDS by air. We have taken away nature's biggest tool, and she's one pissed-off bitch. Make hay when the sun shines, because it's only a matter of time.

A man on a bus once told me the worst-case scenario for humans would be curing cancer. I didn't solicit the opinion; the guy just liked the sound of his own voice. I asked him why he felt this way. He said it's no good to have everyone living to 150. The world can't support it; the economy can't support it. Nature needs a means to an end, and we're robbing it of that. It's all leading up to a big ol' natural ass-whoopin' of humble Homo Sapiens. Eat your vegetables, kids. You're gonna need all the fight you can get.

My pondering of the sidewalk avoidance percentage [S.A.P.] goes right along with this. Somehow nature still has us hierarchied, but hell if we know how it's determined. Someone probably has life figured out, but that someone is hiding out deep in a far-off cave, afraid of the reality of ignorance in the world.

Shortly before Cristen bought the farm, I decided to take a trip. I'm not sure that I ever really *decided,* actually. It was more of a subconscious effort. One morning I woke up and started to sweep my apartment. Two hours later, I'm on Route 3, music blaring, a light drizzle coming down. I didn't know where I was going, but I *did* know where I was heading. I had known for months. Finally, I had broken down, even if I didn't care to admit it to myself.

There are things in this world we accept 'cause we have to: mosquitoes, pinkeye...

There are things in this world we accept because they're part of the unchangeable, necessary system: taxes, vaccination shots...

There are things we accept in this world that we have absolutely no idea why we accept. We do it because everyone else does it and it's the right thing to do. Murder can be like that. Now, I say "can be." Some dumb fuck gets pissed off at work and knifes his kids that night. Well, he might as well skip trial because, due process or not, he's sure as hanged. You see, the legal system is a nice little toy and it makes us feel like we are in control, but the one big, butt-ugly flaw is that it depends on human objectivity, which is about as common as a 10-9 professional soccer game.

Laws don't put people in jail. Crimes don't either. It's the *circumstances* that make the difference. Did the circumstances warrant the act? Self defense, insanity, abortion, manslaughter. All can end up in a death, and it is somehow left to the unfortunate few to separate the excusable from the heinous. What a way to spend a summer—in a hot and sweaty courtroom with a bunch of strangers on hard chairs. With lawyers. And guilty versus innocent? Might as well throw a dart.

Maybe they do. Maybe that's what juries do when they go back into that little room. Maybe a game of cricket decides it all. When they take a really long time to decide, they're playing for points.

I drove for quite a long time. You know you've driven for a while when you suddenly realize you've been listening to gospel music in Spanish for two hours. It's easy to tune out on the long road. It's also easy to crack your car up. Strange how life works. I could end someone's life just by crossing the median. Entire family lives disrupted or ruined. It's much easier to make the front page performing evil than good. The cards are stacked that way forever after you slide down the blood chute into the doctor's awaiting herpetic hands. Go figure, right?

Chapter Nine

That was when I first heard the bees. Just a hum at the time, not yet a buzz. And it was barely noticeable, I tell you.

Chapter Ten

It was past nightfall when I got there. I parked the car alongside the woods, not wanting to attract attention. It was too late now for my purposes. The darkness assured that. I slept a remarkably peaceful sleep.

The sunlight awoke me. It was dawn—dewy, sweet, and innocent. Dixon was a beautiful town. Too pretty to be home to a penitentiary. Yet there it was. No fancy name, just Dixon State Prison. Dixon was one of those places that's a town, a township, and a county all in one. I guess someone just gets lazy in those cases. Either that, or they figure they'd make it easy on everybody.

Steam was coming off the hood of my car. Steam or vapor or smoke. I always confuse those damn things. Chemistry sucks. I reached to my dashboard and grabbed the Styrofoam cup. I tasted the cold and bitter coffee. Just a sip was enough—too much, even. I felt my face, and it was scratchy. I must have been a sight.

Bad situations. Any one of us can fall victim to 'em, and before you know it, your friends start to doubt you, then your family too. Then you get desperate. All this went through my head as I sat there, though it was largely irrelevant. I find it difficult to keep my thoughts under grasp at times. Sometimes it's just easier to let go.

I stared down the hill that morning. The sun was out, and I could hear the chatter of small woodland creatures behind me. It was a comforting sound— summery and cheerful and childlike. There was a smell in the air that I couldn't place at first. It was both pleasant and not. I realized it was hot asphalt. Somewhere, road crews worked, though I thought it a bit early. Probably wanted to avoid the heat of the day. I can't say I blame them. Outdoor work is attractive to the idealistic man, the one who forgets the bitters of winter and the sting of the hot sun.

Down the hillside was the rear of the prison. There was a fenced-in area where the criminals could recreate and dream of long tunnels leading outward.

I didn't know if they'd even let him out there. I knew even less about jails than I did about women. High-risk prisoners, I didn't know where they went. Are they're permanently chained? It was a question to which I hoped never to find the answer. The same hand that had grabbed the coffee now held the steel handle of a knife. I don't know what I planned that day, if anything. I could no more get into the rec. area than the prisoners could get out of it. But I didn't know how to shoot a gun, and that made things difficult. How things have changed.

It ended up a moot point. I never saw him. At least I don't think I did. From my vantage point up on the hill, the cons were essentially tiny talking heads with tattooed shoulders. I remember being quietly happy not to have seen him. After all, vengeance solves nothing. Jill would still be gone.

Somewhere else, deeper and more subtly, I wished he stood in front of my car even as I sat there. I imagined blood spatter on the windshield and a dent in the bumper. Not a large dent; I would steamroll rather than smack. I wanted to see the whites of his eyes. Still, this feeling was very subdued. I reached in the glove box and drew out an unopened cigarette pack.

I removed the cellophane, got out of my sedan, and took a seat on the roof of my car. As I smoked one, two, three butts. Yes, yes, we all can slip, all right? I looked back at the woods—fresh, green, and youthful—thinking of the creatures within its treed walls. I could only hope they were happy in their simple lives. I wanted to hurt somebody.

Eventuality Avoidance. 1.n. The often subconscious use of day-to-day, inane activities as a means of averting thoughts concerning meaning, consequence, and the unknown in this lifetime. See *escapism.* [1955-60]

Hegemony is a wonderful thing. The best kind of control is that which those under control think is natural, or part of an unchangeable system.

Ad in the Barton Press: *Had enough. Even as you live, you die. Goods to be dispersed. Good riddance.*

Graffitied on a stone wall, Madison, WI: *Death is a reward, long life a punishment.*

And still the hum got louder. Slowly louder. Nearly buzzy, but not quite.

Chapter Eleven

My writing has been scattered; for this I apologize. The medication is making it hard to concentrate. Hyperbole comes easily to me when I'm stoned. I am feeling better today; that should help.

I caught a glimpse of myself in the mirror this morning. The white shirt I wore contrasted sharply with the circles under my eyes and my black, scraggly beard. I don't look a bit like the child of long ago who jumped and skipped and frolicked. That seems like a lifetime ago, when I thought adulthood would bring total understanding and omnipotence. A lifetime ago, at least. That was before the advertising companies ate away at my brain. The same business that made me a relative fortune has sucked away my soul, leaving me as another empty shell ready to be refilled by Madison Avenue's minions. Like you, I am tortured in the shower by inane jingles. Like you, I pay other people to front their products on my threads. I figure it was worth the trade-off; advertising bought me a really good shower with lots of hot, high, and high-pressure jets.

I realize I told you that the man on the bus—the one with the cancer cure theory—liked to run his mouth. In truth, I've been running my own as well. It seems best to let the story tell itself, so my soapbox is now officially pushed firmly and forever back beneath my bed. It joins the dust bunnies in the darkness. Again, I apologize.

Soon after I returned from my little trip up north, I decided I needed a vacation. At this point, Cristen and I were becoming serious, and I felt it was time we got away to face life from a new perspective and begin to create some new and fresh memories for ourselves. Every new relationship should be granted its own slate. Too much baggage is being carried around, if you ask me, or even if you don't.

We decided to go to the lake, to rough it for a weekend of sun and fun or vice versa.

We took her truck. It had four-wheel drive and was sufficiently beaten upon for a trip into the deep wood. We decided not to look for a commercial campsite, opting instead to take the more mellow and private option of hiking off the highway until we found a site we liked. Opson Lake is rather large, and though it draws quite a crowd in the summer months, there is enough circumference land so that folks may be assured solitude should they search for it.

I packed a grill—the same one we used for the concert—on loan from Pat. There were fishing poles, two sleeping bags since we didn't own a double, a three-man tent, a large cooler of food, a smaller cooler of beer, and a couple of bright orange rafts—all the makings of a hell of a weekend. I brought a knife with me whenever I camped. Normal people use them to fillet fish and prepare food, but really I'm terrified of bears. Admittedly, what good a four-inch knife would do against a grizzly, I don't know.

It didn't start off as we had hoped. There was a torrential downpour that evening, and what's worse, I had numb-headedly left the tent stakes in my closet. Not that it mattered in the end, as the rain meant there would be two bodies available to hold down the fort, literally.

We sat by flashlight that night. It lacks the romantic essence of candlelight, but it's a lot safer in a tent. The thunder outside was crisp and harsh, and loud enough to shake the land around us. It was the type of gripping storm that raises your adrenaline and brings your innermost fears to the surface. It reminds you that, yes, you are still afraid of the dark and all the things that go bump in the night. When the wind howls or the silence cuts like a knife, we are forced from our protective shells into a chilling world where we don't know the rules and our irrational emotions rule the roost. Thunder is the set of headlights that glides across the wall in the dead of night when we sleep at faraway hotels. It is the slow drip from the kitchen faucet when we're alone in bed at night. It doesn't pull punches, and it backs itself up with bolts of hard-core, unrelenting electricity. I digress.

We got very drunk. Along with the beer, we packed a bottle of whiskey we never planned on using but which circumstances dictated we finish, and finish it we did. A smart camper always brings along some token item to kill time in case of inclement weather, and we had done just that. We had a 13-inch television, black-and-white, and we watched a baseball game which extended into the thirteenth inning. I was surprised that we had reception, but you know what they say about gift horses.

Cristen was a far bigger sports fan than myself, but I must admit, watching it there with her as rain pelted our tent, I was rather enamored with the game. It ended when the third baseman drove a ball into right-center, bringing in the man on third who had doubled and then moved along on a sac bunt.

I must admit also that I had to ask Cristen to explain the infield fly rule at one point.

I didn't feel like much of a man doing so, a fact I find interesting looking back. I asked why the infield fly rule didn't go into effect with just one man on base. Cristen explained that assuming the batter busts it out of the box on the pop-up, he should easily coast into first base, eliminating the con-job double play that the infield fly rule is designed to prevent in the first place. I'm still fuzzy on it, I'm afraid, but I nodded my head as she explained, because I'm sure that no one alive could have done a better job of it. She tried to explain all the rules to me at an earlier date. She had one of those thick books with black-and-white illustrations that are labeled *Figure 3A*. I tried to go along with it and learn about a game that was foreign to me, but it just didn't want to stick.

The television was turned off at 9:45 p.m.. It still rained hard, and when I peeked my head out to take a look towards the lake down the slope, I could see bolts of lightning coming fast and furious and breaking into three, four forks. I felt total serenity at that point. I remember thinking how very conceivable it is that ancient civilizations should think up myths to explain natural forces.

These myths are often laughed at today, but it would seem they are as good an explanation as any, and they make for much more fanciful tales. Giant crabs in the ocean and snakes that swim among the clouds. Kind of fanciful, really. Makes you wish for a more interesting world than one under the power of electricity and motion. Very efficient, but not so much in the glamour department.

Cristen and I made love under the stars, even if we were inside the tent. The electricity in the air and the natural thrill granted by a hard storm made it an especially frisky session. We were alone, with only the yellow, haunting eyes of the forest inhabitants upon us. I could hear the rain fall off severely, and there was the sound of raccoon chatter at the lake shore.

I remember reading that raccoons adore the taste of crawfish, or is it crayfish? Truthfully, I'm not sure there's a difference, and I sure as hell don't know if Lake Opson has either of them. But the masked bandits must have found something that was to their liking, 'cause they were shrieking up a storm down there. Food could be one explanation for that. The other's a good woman. Maybe one of those big fellas found himself a gal and the two were now getting acquainted. I could relate.

When we awoke, the weather had seen a great improvement. The sun's rays scattered brightly across the surface of the lake, and reflected through the forests, dancing on the leaves of the larger trees. The sky was a bright, intoxicating hue of blue, like a big bowl of, well, blue gelatin. The air was crisp, and you could feel a breeze under your armpits. If this wasn't a perfect day, then I have never had the pleasure of seeing one.

Cristen and I did a little shuffling, removing all the beer from the small cooler except for a six-pack. We made a couple of sandwiches, which joined the beer in the little cooler. Armed with food, drink, and with fishing poles stretched across our backs, we waded out into the lake.

There was a pier about 500 feet to our right, but we chose instead to set our sights on a large rock which protruded from the lake about forty feet out.

The natural setting felt more soulful, and who knows what monstrosities the local fishermen might have left on the dock?

The boulder was flattened on its top, making for an ideal place to suntan and take it all in. A third person would have cramped its surface, but for a couple, it was terrific.

We had taken in several small fish, maybe six total—nothing keepable—when we ran out of beer. Besides, you can only sit on a rock for so long. We now treaded the exposed stones toward the shore, and were about halfway there when hell ascended upon us.

I happened to be looking downward (assward) at the time, so I saw it well. Cristen was wearing sandals, and the water had made her footing a bit tense. Finally, almost inevitably, her left sandal slid out from beneath her. I will never forget seeing her ankle dislocate. Her foot was at a right angle to the leg, and for a brief instant she was actually standing on the base of her calf. I didn't hear any rip or tear. Instead, for just a moment, the whole world went dead silent.

It was the instant between paradise and hell, the moment of the dawning realization. In the time it took for the pain to go from ankle to brain, my own mind realized this event marked the end of any fun we'd be having this weekend. It was something I realized in a resentful manner, as if the accident were planned to take away a bit of joy from my life. The funny thing, though, is that I didn't stop enjoying myself at that moment. Nothing of the sort, actually.

Chapter Twelve

S he screamed. It was a loud, piercing-to-the-point-of-curdling-the-blood, horrifying scream. It echoed through the valley, off the rocks. I knew she would not be able to keep her balance, and indeed she didn't. Heroically, she stood as damaged goods atop that rock for several seconds, screaming, until pain totally enveloped her, forcing her to submit. I never would have been able to hold my balance so long. Weaker sex my ass.

I remember the look on her face at that moment. I remember it clearly, actually. The moment was one of those that plays out as if in slow motion and then lingers in your head until the day you die. Her lips receded, baring her teeth, small and shiny. Her eyes rolled up to the point where her irises were little half melons resting on a bed of eyeball. Her face was white, and not the good alabaster white that you read about in all of the old-time dramatic plays. This white was ashen, defeated, dead.

Then she fell backward. Slowly, symmetrically, and into four feet of water.

Up until this point, I had been frozen in a curious, thoughtful, disbelieving pose. At last, fear released its hold on my body, and I sprang into motion. I stepped from my rock to hers—far more successfully than she had—and reached blindly for her ankle. Her head was bobbing at this point, dipping momentarily beneath the water's surface and then popping up into the daylight. It was impossible to tell the tears from the lake water.

I looked around at my surroundings. It was indeed a large lake, with many people around it. Where were they now? Why weren't they responding to the screaming? The opposite shore was far away. Would the sound even carry that far? Our side was more isolated; favored by the locals. I looked at our campsite and realized that the outgrowth of trees over the water acted as a physical barrier.

Still, I was sure that plenty of people heard the screams, meaning one of two things. On one hand, it's possible, perhaps, that people assumed the screams to be shrieks of fun. Children's voices can get pretty high when they're alive with pleasure. Little girls can rival dog whistles. I wasn't buying this particular theory, but I was trying like hell to think myself into it. Because the other possibility is that nobody cared. Or at least that they didn't want to help if it meant the possibility of risk to themselves.

Besides, there were hot dogs to be eaten, softballs to be tossed.

I must admit, I've been subjected to this phenomenon myself. You hear a scream, a cry for help, you figure, "Ah, someone else will take care of it." And they usually do, because there are two or three good people left, although they are usually overlooked. I like to think they prefer it that way.

So that was it. Either people misidentified the scream, or they just didn't want to care. Help hinders, right? We must learn to help ourselves. Only the strong survive. Nice guys finish last. Give 110%. There are far too many clichés in world. Life can't be summed up in a blurb, or maybe it can and I'm too scared of what it would mean to admit to it. Maybe I've just eaten one too many fortune cookies, though I doubt that's possible. Those suckers are good.

My hand was around her good ankle. I reached at first for her left leg because it was closer, but thankfully, I realized my mistake before I brought a fistful of pain upon her. I might well have pulled her foot off. No, I had her right ankle, and I would bring her ashore. Even if she was unconscious, I could place her in the truck and drive the thirteen miles to the hospital. After all, she didn't look well, and she would be on crutches for a while, but the injury was by no means life-threatening. It was only as scary as it was because we were in the middle of West Nowhere.

I would drag her ashore and lay her on the dirt while I drove the truck to the lake's edge. Then I would take her to that hospital, and she would recover her strength, and we would cut the trip short and eat dinner on the couch while watching old movies on the television. Tomorrow was 99-cent night at Goldfin Video, if she preferred a rental. Everything would be O.K.

Except that's not what happened.

The buzz grew. It had been rising steadily but slowly, but now it grew by leaps and bounds.

The mind is capable of performing an incredible feat. It can process a phenomenal amount of information in a relatively brief time. We take in our surroundings, feed the information through the sorter, and make decisions almost instantaneously. We take it all for granted because we do it thousands of times a day, far more still should we be driving. Well, the scene at the lake probably took less than a minute, but in that small space of time my own mind processed thoughts, made decisions, and in the process changed my life forever.

My first thought was of Thelma Vicaro. She was a girl I knew in high school. Well, "knew" might not be the most appropriate word here. Few people really knew her, but this is not a story of popular or unpopular. Popularity is irrelevant here. Thelma was different. She appeared unaffected by the questions that concern a typical junior year class—who was dating who? when was Homecoming?—all of the usual fanfare.

She did well in her classes, but kind of crept from room to room and locker to locker. She seemed to bounce through her life like an ice-cream stick floating down a street, bopping along the rain-laden gutter until it eventually disappears down a sewer hole into a black oblivion, forgotten to all but the very small minority. L.I.F.E. And then nothing. Fade to black. No rabbit in this hat.

One day I saw Thelma bop-bopping through the hallway, almost invisible. It had become an obsession of mine to figure out how this girl did it. How she could withstand such isolation and exist within her own world? On this particular day, I realized I could wait no longer for an answer. I approached her, nearly knocking her over. I don't think she was used to being approached. I excused myself for my intrusion into her space, beat around the bush for a while, and finally got my nerve up.

"How do you do it, Thelma?"

"Do what?" She didn't even look up. Even then she was...elsewhere.

"You live in your own world. Don't you *care*? Isn't there anything you like? Why do you act like... like...?" At this point, I realized I was being driven by curious angst built up over three years. I hadn't taken the time to actually develop a question, and now that the time was here, I was going nowhere.

"...I'm dead?"

Those were her words; I remember them well.

"I guess. I'm not trying to sound mean. I was just...curious."

She looked at me, finally, as if wondering whether to open up to a stranger. I guess I made the cut. Like I said, I don't possess a threatening look.

"You are born into a world not of your choosing, with no hint as to what direction to move in. Your parents are chosen for you. Your friends *you* choose, but most of them you actually have little in common with. The association exists to make you feel... secure." The speech was well versed. Obviously I wasn't the only person to have asked the question. Or maybe she had just been craving an opportunity to vomit her thoughts. She continued.

"None of us has any idea what's going on, but we each develop our own way to make it look like we do— spirituality, pompous academia... Or we find a way to escape it." She paused for air. At last I got a word in.

"So this is your way of...escaping?"

"No." She paused to look at the clock above me. I'm not sure she was actually checking the time. She might just have been collecting her thoughts. She had the look of someone about to make a serious decision. Finally, she continued.

"No. It's just that I don't waste my time trying to find answers when I don't even know the question."

"Kind of a fatalistic attitude."

"Far from it. I spend my time learning, observing, making mistakes. It's a sacrifice."

"How so?" I was surprised to find her to be so open, considering she could not have had much practice with conversation. For a second, I thought it was a sign of wisdom and confidence, but perhaps in the end Thelma *was* lonely. Maybe this *was* just her own means of escape. She put her foot up against the row of lockers, staring into space across the hallway. Classes were over now, and papers were strewn on the floor. I wondered if I would miss my bus, or Thelma hers. She probably wouldn't care.

"I'm from a poor family, Ed." She knew my name. I was surprised. "I have two shitty parents, and I can't do any one thing particularly well. And I'm stupid."

"You're not stupid, Thelma."

"I am."

"No. I mean, anyone who devotes this much thought to..."

"It's irrelevant. It doesn't help my situation in life, so it doesn't count as an asset. I'm stupid by society's terms, and therefore I'm stupid." I was fighting a losing battle here. But I had one more question.

"You said your life was a sacrifice?"

"Yes. My odds aren't good here, Ed. I know it. I'll never make it here. I don't...fit. So I'm learning what I can from the shadows, and I'll use it in the next world. I'll rock that world."

It was a strange mentality, and I thought it to be a string of bullshit. At least, that is, until I heard that she killed herself three years later. So either she was really lonely or really gutsy. If there is a second world, I hope Thelma's rocking it. Still, I think of her. I think of what she said, and I find myself agreeing far too often.

I find it hard to find the good in people. Sometimes life seems to be a manipulative chess match with a whole lot of back stabbing. You can't trust anybody, and the bad far outweighs the good. And it's when I feel this way that I hear the buzzing, when the sky can't be blue enough to ease my mind. And, like I said, it's been getting louder, which takes us back to the day by the lake. Maybe you're not ready to get back to that tale yet, but I can only hope that the story of Thelma will help explain my mindset. I can only hope that you understand. I can only hope that you are *like us*.

Because...the buzzing was there at the lake, disturbing the peace of the day. God forgive me.

I don't feel an ounce of guilt concerning Thelma's young death. I've rarely even thought about it, to be truthful. Maybe I could have told somebody, and maybe they could have stopped her (though I doubt it), but why deny a person their dream? Like I said, you have to give those people credit. Anyway, she's in a better place now; I'm sure of it.

Chapter Thirteen

(Fuck superstition. Bloody Mary,
Bloody Mary, Bloody Mary.)

I reached for my knife, sheathed in a leather case attached to my belt. I don't know *why* I reached for it initially. Perhaps I subconsciously hoped that I'd finally get some good old-fashioned masculine use out of the damn thing. Up till then, it had mostly served as a carry-along. It had a smooth black handle, marked with a small silver star at the base of the shaft. Gleaming in the sunlight, the blade looked larger than it actually was.

I took the knife in my hand and sliced into Cristen's ankle. I think I wanted to end it. I wanted the screaming and the madness to stop so that we could retreat to our tranquil weekend, perhaps even catch another on-air ball game. I was beginning to like that strategy. My actions at the lake only made the screams worse, and the effect was cyclical. I *really* wanted the situation to end, so I buried the knife.

I plunged the four-inch blade into her breast, which was not quite as easy a task as you might imagine. Besides the psychological block, the body isn't nearly as fragile as we make it out to be. Normally I would never have been able to get past the initial stab. It turned my stomach. However, I was no longer acting rationally. I was now at the mercy of adrenaline and emotion, an elixir that acts a lot like excessive alcohol. I stabbed repeatedly.

The screaming stopped. Perhaps had she been able to look up into my eyes, to instill a sense of guilt and a sense of '*why?*' perhaps then I could have stopped. Maybe she still could have been saved. I guess she would no longer have been my friend after that, so I would have lost Jill either way. Cristen.

It doesn't matter, though, because she didn't look up at me. She had lost consciousness. I don't know if she swallowed water or passed out from shock or if I had pierced a lung, though I doubt it was the latter because she let out an awful scream which really put a jump into me. She didn't look at me, and I never had the privilege of a last glimpse into those feeling, moving eyes. I do, however, remember her hair shimmering in the bright sunlight, wet with lake water.

The slice on her calf actually bled more than the chest wounds. I retrieved my knife and threw it into the lake. Had my mind been clearer, I would not have done this, because even though *I* knew I was no murderer, the cops might not be so quick to buy it. If my mind had been clear, I might also not have released her body. I let it sit there, perhaps with a guilty conscience, hoping whatever would come of this, it would come quickly.

I didn't hurry off. Instead I sat and wept at the evil in the world. The true evildoers—the Jeffrey Simonses—bring shame to the rest of us who might be so unlucky as to find circumstances of heartache, angst, and unfortunate coincidence. Our actions are judged by their intent. Even the holiest of men might steal bread were his family starving, but our laws don't always see things that way. They ignore extraordinary circumstances and befriend hard facts. What can I say? It's a complicated, fast-paced world we live in; sometimes hard and fast lines must be drawn in the sand. I had the feeling that I had just stepped over one of them. This is why I wept. I wept for the world. I wept for reason, and passion, and love.

I sat there for what must have been twenty minutes. The thought that the fish and the parasites and the insects might find my lover tasty was too much to bear. Just hours ago we had been in passionate embrace, and now there was a psychological universe between us. She knew things now that I did not, and may never. At last, she was back in the hands of God, which are soft and warm and tender. God has hands like blue jeans fresh from the dryer.

Finally, I rose from my place on the rock, shook the water from my jeans, and stumbled shoreward. I had collected my thoughts, and now there was work to be done. Not that I knew what my next move was supposed to be. They don't hand out manuals for this situation when you're in the Scouts. You learn how to tie knots and build fires and survive with only a fishhook, but no one can educate you as to how to survive a loss of innocence.

There are nations and cultures in this world-which have very real and obvious rites of passage into manhood. America lacks this. Sure, there's the old driver's license, the loss of one's virginity, but these thing are more about getting old than growing up. That day at the lake was my personal rite of passage. My life was about to change, for obvious reasons, but beyond that, I knew I was now enlightened. I was learning a life lesson.

I took one last look at my lover, who'd been cleansed by the air and water. She looked so innocent, and I must admit, at that time I had a pang of guilt. If only I could have those precious moments back! I forced my gaze from her body, and had to stop myself from glancing over my shoulder on the walk up to camp. She was no longer Cristen. She was a body, I reminded myself, and that body would serve to nurture the natural world. It's all part of the plan. Bacteria need to eat.

I could not help thinking, though, how many men that body had known, how many children that smile had made happy, how many friends had gained pleasure from the person who now lied limp by the rock in the lake. I wondered exactly how long it takes before the body starts to stiffen with rigor mortis. Could it have set in already? How quickly does the blood pool? If I touched her, would she (it?) feel human? I was tempted to go back to her corpse—how often do we have the chance to touch death, to shake its hand, dare I say to make love to it? I resisted the urge splendidly.

I rolled the tent up clumsily, wrapping it crepe fashion around most of our supplies. I threw the whole mess in the back of the truck, cleaned camp, and made myself a bagel with cream cheese.

The ride out of the woods was tremendously bumpy. I was not driving my own vehicle, and frankly,

I don't think I'm all that good with a stick shift. I mean, really, who can think about three pedals and a stick all at once? I had opened a soda and placed it in between my legs. It spilled over when the truck hit one particularly high bump. The contents of the can spilled on my pants, and I found myself wishing I had packed one of those lemony sodas instead of the grape stuff. I looked awfully silly with a purple crotch. Purple is not a flattering color at all. I cursed aloud, just as I would have if someone were beside me. For some reason, cursing makes us feel better. I cursed a lot in those days. Fuck yeah.

I abandoned the truck outside of town in a parking lot. I used a tarp to cover the goods in the bed, and left the keys in the ignition. I hoped that someone else would get some use out of the pickup. It had quite a few miles of exploring left in it. Now that I think of it, they probably auctioned it off when the shit hit the fan, meaning that some lowbrow businessman probably bought it cheap and is now using it to haul around patio furniture. Hardly a fitting use for such a beautiful machine. Too many people buy off-road cars for on-road lives. I thought about Cristen's body again. It must have been warming in the afternoon sun. I wondered if it would smell. I had to remind myself that she was in a better place. Oh, why did she have to hurt herself?

By this time, I had walked three blocks to the bus depot. It wasn't really a depot, but a sidewalk stop without so much as a glass enclosure to protect you from the weather. It wasn't too long before the 72 pulled up. One thing about these parts: they sure have a fine system of public transportation. I don't know where they got the money. Taxes around there were low, and most people had cars anyway. At the time though, I was thankful that someone had made the effort. I put my buck-fifty in the slot, thankful I had the exact change. Bus drivers get all crabby about that. I suppose I would, too, if I had to deal with people asking for change of a fifty all day long.

The bus pulled away from the curb amid a cloud of blue smoke, chugging along with its 40-odd passengers until I finally reached home.

I went inside and slept. This might come as a surprise, but I slept deeply and restfully. I was at peace.

Chapter Fourteen

"**K**iller" bees were introduced purposefully. An accident gave them their opportunity to wreak havoc upon the natural order in the western hemisphere, but their initial introduction into South America was very much planned. The problem in this case was control. The idea was to breed a bee that would provide increased honey production—a clear benefit for the human harvester. But as often happens when people attempt to manipulate their environment, *something* happened.

The bees inevitably got loose, worked their way out of Brazil and through Latin America, and eventually crossed the border into the American Southwest. Now, don't let the media buzz mislead you.

This is the same media who portray sharks as evil man-killers who take lives for sheer joy. This is a media without a soul. Still, there is a clear story here. The bees themselves aren't much to look at, but well over one hundred people have died as a result of human tampering in this case alone. Over and over, the natural world has cast its hard, gray eyes in our direction and stated in a stern voice, "Don't fuck with me." Clearly, we should have learned by now. But we all need to make our own mistakes.

Following this theme, I remember vividly that it was at this point in time—just after dumping the pickup—that I got *the idea*, an idea that would forever change my status in the world. I cannot fully explain the reasoning behind it now. I can only give you sound bites. Frankly, you lack the capacity to understand in total.

This might sound a bit presumptuous, or even arrogant, but I mean no ill will. Truth is, that's just the way it is. More than likely, you are a 98-percenter. All I can tell you is that it made sense at the time. My idea was based in fact, though I admit I might have gone about it in the wrong fashion.

Time is short now; there is no room for further diversion. In the interest of future generations, let's begin. Oh, one thing. Before it gets involved, I recommend you get a soda, Doctor. Soda is sweet and satisfying and taken for granted, and it might well be your last. Use a straw. Feel free to dribble its goodness down your chin. And for God's sake, cherish every sip.

I left the body and ditched the truck. Now I was asleep. It was during this serene period of unconscious bliss that I achieved the next level. And like so many good and revolutionary ideas in this lifetime, it all began with a dream.

Chapter Fifteen

E volution is a driving force. From what I'm told, it works in two ways. Two beautifully designed (?) and awesomely simple ways. If you are familiar with these methods, skip ahead. It is, after all, in your best interest to conserve time. Life is short. For the dummies in the audience—yourself included—I'll continue.

The first of the two ways is methodical to the point that it almost appears planned. Religious folk among you might argue that it *is* planned, and I'm not about to tell you that you're wrong. Who am I to argue the God issue? You might say, for instance, that God, or some such, planted fossils and other evidence as temptation to ditch your faith. But whether this is the case or not, such evidence of evolution *does* exist, and that fact is damn hard to argue. Natural selection is beyond the control of humans. I'll let it do its thing. It's the *other* changing force that I'm concerned with.

Mutation.

It's natural selection's wittier, faster moving, more devious brother. It robs Peter to pay Paul. It's the friend that stabs you in the back. It's the recessive gene on cocaine. It's the knockout, shit-kicking, earthshaking force that's impossible to contend with. It acts swiftly and changes everything. Mutation makes for change in a hurry, often too fast to be counteracted efficiently. This is when whole species die off, when they can't find a way to combat change.

Albinism is a mutation. Now, I'm not mocking albino people, snakes, or woodland creatures. They have as much right to live as the rest of us. But when placed alone, out on the prairie, out in the wild, albinism in and of itself is a dreadful survival disadvantage. It leaves you without camouflage, without resistance to the rays of the afternoon sun. And it's just one example. Now, sometimes mutations make for a disadvantage, such as in the case of albinism. But sometimes not... and that's the problem.

We've come too far too fast. I, for one, will not sit back and see mutation—evolution's dishwater—work to strip away our progress. Language, agriculture, industry. Much as I hate my fellow man, these are brilliant advances. I'd like to see them furthered. And that's why I was born—me and my fellow one-percenters. To reestablish natural selection without compromising human progress.

Ninety-eight percent of you mean nothing. You were born to live long enough to fuck, to breed, to pass your genes. What you learn in your lifetime might be significant to you, but it means nothing to the world at large. One percent of you—or thereabouts...scientists still argue about the numbers—are mutators. You bring rapid change. Your genes are special. Don't go out celebrating yet. Change isn't always good.

At least your lives have true meaning though. Most people are as crucial to the fate of the world as paper doilies.

Then there's the remaining one percent. We're nature's goalies. I'd name you some people who were on this list, but I fear it's too dangerous. They were people who were ahead of their time. Most of them you would despise because their ideas weren't quite *right*. At least not from a sociological, let's-all-get-along mentality.

Biologically speaking, though, their ideas were genius. They were structured to eliminate harmful elements. The changes they created came either passively, as a result of biological mutation (the old standard), or through ideas, which are essentially as biological as genes themselves. Ideas are what make people people. I *will* tell you one thing: the person you're thinking of, he wasn't a one-percenter.

Mutation drives diversity, which is good. If a creature gets too comfortable in its makeup, nature will catch up to it. Diversity means resistance to disease, decay, and destruction. Generally. The real trouble is when mutation takes an ugly wrong turn.

That's where we one-percenters come in. We clean up the mess when nature "makes a mistake." We put out the fire. Nature's relief pitchers. I realized this after Cristen's unfortunate demise.

Until I hit the pillow at home, I wondered how my mind could have frozen as it did. How could I have allowed myself to take the life of a good friend and lover? The dream provided the answer. I was working for a greater good than myself. I was working for the human race as a whole. Representing, as the young folk say. And it was time now for me to fulfill my destiny and discover the true meaning of life.

Chapter Sixteen

Cristen was essentially a good person. She was fun and intelligent and caring. But she had bad genes. I guess I figured this out the same way those bastards sense my submissiveness when they head toward me on the sidewalk. It's not logical or rational. My foreknowledge concerning Cristen's future effect on the world came instinctually. She was the first; she took the longest to figure out. The others wouldn't fool me so well. I hung on with Cristen for a long time because I resisted and because I had been in love. I vowed not to make that mistake again. I didn't want to admit my place in the world, but the dream was far too strong to fight. Business has to come first when you're a savior. And let there be no mistaking it, that's exactly what I am.

I felt confident. I had fate on my side. I was careful, though, especially in the beginning. I could not be certain that the fact that I was a force of good necessarily made me less expendable. Even at only one percent of the population, there was still a hell of a lot of us, going purely by numbers. I didn't know how far nature would go to protect me. What I had learned now, finally, was the reason behind my superb intelligence. I would never own the world, but I would help define the parameters of its existence.

The best part was that there were others out there who felt just like me. I wondered how to meet them. I wondered if I would now recognize my coworkers by sight. My dream was a revelation, and I couldn't be sure what else had changed in my life or in my capacity for power. Suddenly I felt immune to the smaller issues and tribulations that worry normal people. Liquor could no longer hold me hostage. Cigarettes could not cancer me. Why would nature waste resources to kill one of its own? The only thing I had to fear was my own kind, and possibly my own mind should I not keep it together. The alcohol helped there, too.

I needed to look the part. Someone in my prominent position should not look like a businessman. I wanted to look like an agent of nature. It was necessary for me to become objective, transient, and unnoticeable. I traded the loafers for sandals. I cut my hair very short. I took to standard blue button-down tee-shirts. It was no time for pride in one's self. My own ego had to take a back seat to the welfare of society at large. We had grown too big for our britches, and I was the atom bomb that never was. I was part of the *P\ pièce de résistance* in a changing and mysterious world.

To whom did I owe this great honor? Is this why I suffered as an ugly and unpopular kid and then as an ugly and unpopular man? Was it all just to create a sense of discipline and objectivity within me? I felt sure of it. Suddenly I felt terribly empowered. Everything began to make sense. I stayed in the apartment for two days, and then I packed a bag.

Normal possessions were useless and irrelevant to me now. The rules had changed, and items such as photos, knickknacks and thingamajigs would only weigh me down. I spent one full night cradling my most precious and longest-owned possessions. I needed to get it out of my system. Finally I packed my bag with the items that would serve me and my objective: booze and cigarettes. I needed to stay calm, and—short of prescription drugs—smokes and booze are the best tranqs you can get. I first packed a large duffel bag, but I felt this would slow me down too much. There might be people after me. Some might not understand. There are a lot of naive fucks in the world—the same people who are locking normal people in asylums and buying thirty-dollar underwear.

The bees are now in Arizona, and they sound eerily familiar.

I also packed a gun. It wasn't mine, as you might have surmised by now. Jill insisted we keep one in the house, just as her father had kept one in the McIntyre residence. Jill's mother had been attacked in the home before the children were born, while her husband was away. After that time, a firearm was the rule. I had only seen Jill hold the gun during the moving process, and I'm not even sure she could shoot straight. But it made her feel comfortable. I must say, though, it's truly surreal mentioning a pure dove such as Jill in the same sentence as a means of violent death.

I took the gun along because I also had to be able to protect myself, especially now. It was about time that a young man learned to fire when fired upon. Talk about a rite of passage. Still, the weapon felt alien in my grip.

People like Jeffrey Simons do the rest of us a terrible injustice. These bastards do things for kicks, and suddenly all the world's people are labeled liars, crooks, or killers. Murder is only murder when it robs the world of innocence. These are all very fine lines. The difference between sex and rape, after all, is both nothing and everything in the world. The penetration is there, but...the intent is not. And it all comes down to intent. Simons had selfish, evil intent. The work my brothers and I do is done to weed out the sick, the weak-gened, the ill-minded. We are here to act in nature's stead now that the political, over-structured world has tied its hands.

We are the panacea, and we are not to be denied. Not by you or your laws or your military. You can't scare us off with weapons, and you can't weird us out with poetry slams. We will not be intimidated by women's groups or animal rights activists or vigilante justice. Move aside, citizen, lest ye become an innocent victim. Do not step in the crossfire, Samaritan, for there will always be another bullet. The apocalypse is upon us, and heaven knows we are your only defense. Fuck Jeffrey Simons and his self-minded fanaticism.

Jill would understand this. She understood everything. She was a force of good in a way that I could never dream. She was out planting flowers, damn it. Where's the harm in that? But she could only do so much, and that is truly the ironic part. Try as she might, she could never change the world. Her good deeds caused smiles; they didn't save lives. Goodness is pansy power. Real power lies in science. Never mind what people tell you; penicillin still cures more people than love.

Love soothes the soul, but leaves the body flat.

I remember when she would cry. She didn't do it often, which might come as a surprise. She was all things feminine, but she didn't cry often. I think it's because she never held back her emotion to begin with, she never bottled up. Thus, there was no need for this great release from time to time. Crying, after all, is just a physical defense, and maybe a form of communication, though I doubt that very much. I saw Jill cry at funerals and during two mushy movies. Other than that, I can't recall. Maybe I've already mentioned another instance. Hell if I remember. I have been writing for an awfully long time now, and I'm still waiting patiently.

There is nothing that tears at a man quite like seeing a woman cry. It is draining and frustrating and leaves you feeling helpless. When Jill did cry, it was truly a sight to behold. Her iridescent eyes would wince, and her nose would tweak like that of a rabbit. It hurts to see a woman cry, but the beauty contained in the shine of her eyes and the curl of her lips would almost make you wish she'd cry more often; it was that moving a sight.

Chapter Seventeen

I took to the woods, for two reasons. First, I felt sure that they would soon discover Cristen's body. Some snot-nosed brat would be out with his snot-nosed friend. They'd be hunting or fishing or shooting up at the lake. By that, I mean they'd be "shooting" up at the lake, not "shooting up" at the lake. English sucks. One of the lads would have the misfortune of tripping over her fish-bitten corpse. It's always the same. Joe and Jack Dumbfuck are out on an innocent hike when they happen to come across a decaying body. They ponder the situation (i.e. search the body for money and jewelry) before finally placing an anonymous call to the police. It's funny what we do anonymously. It's the ultimate cop-out, but it does a lot of good for the world.

It would happen soon, I was sure of it. Those woods were heavily used, and wasn't like I'd made any extra effort to conceal what I had done. We only conceal that which we are ashamed of, like little dogs who piss the carpet.

The second reason for my escape into the woods was equally practical. I was now a force of nature, and I thought it only right that I be closer to my benefactor. I no longer wanted to subject myself to the influence of my global society—a society that has practiced genocide and held slaves. Think about that for a moment. Fewer than 200 years ago, slavery was a state-sanctioned institution. It was the norm. How can I ever take seriously the moral statements of any people who would hold their own as captives? It perplexes me to consider the fact that some folks consider humans to be basically good creatures. I spit in those people's faces.

So I took my bag of treats and I ran far, far away. It was time to get down and dirty. It was time to do my duty.

Chapter Eighteen

I can't say that the decision was an easy one. My first thought was of Mrs. Edwards, the wife of that asshole teacher I was telling you about. Like I said, she deserved it. I went as far as to ascertain her last known address, or at least the last known address I had the ability to get my hands on.

Two things stopped me. For the first part, there was a good chance she'd be dead by now. And even if she wasn't, she'd surely be old, frail, and feeble-minded. There's no challenge in that. She'd probably be offering me cookies even as I slipped the noose around her wrinkly, crusty neck. I shudder at the thought of old peoples' necks.

Secondly, and ultimately more important, was the integrity of my new position. There is a certain amount of honor which needs to be maintained when one is given a measure of responsibility. I wasn't about to take such a position for granted by striking down some balding idiot just because he cut me off at a green arrow.

No, more thought would be necessary. For a while, I considered random acts of terror. Perhaps allowing fate to decide things with a simple flip through the phone book. Somehow, that didn't suit me. I'd have as good a chance of knocking off a strong, glowing force as I would have of taking out some lowlife, parasitic bloodworm.

The narcissism factor was admittedly a challenge. I had always been ugly, weak, slow-minded. Here was an opportunity for cold revenge, the dream of every small boy ever to be picked last in a gym-class roundup. I even came up with a fantasy. I imagined eyeing a well-built, smart-looking man at the grocery store... some slug who would no doubt have garnered favor in the locker room. I'd follow him and his waspish, one-too-many-times-under-the-knife, dye-streaked wife back to their million-dollar home and hold them both at gunpoint. At that time I'd force the wife to strip, and have relations with her while the strapping beau stood by, watching impotent and red-faced. Yeah, I'd get her all turned on, too, you bet I would.

I'd tie him to the banister, naked but for a pair of his old lady's best pink skivvies. That's the way I'd love the cops to find him: shamed, powerless, and beaten at his own game of humiliation. Maybe I'd leave him his wife's fingers to remember me by. And two nipples for good luck. Milk the situation, so to speak. Pardon me, I'm not much of a funnyman. I am here to tell a story for posterity and for whatever help it might afford you in future assessment of the world at large. Sometimes in school, I'd be mocked for my attempts at wit. We all have to try, because if we can't make the people around us laugh, what good are we? What good are we even if we can?

As it was, I took the high road and maintained my own quiet honor.

Paul Stark was my choice instead.

He wasn't a C.E.O. That would have been too easy a choice. Rather, he was a guy in the wrong place at the wrong time with a stupid look on his face. I should have made a choice based on fact and reason, but I did not. Rather, I went on instinct, and when considering a decision involving primality and livelihood, perhaps this is the perfect way to heads/tails it.

I didn't know him. I didn't know he had four children. I didn't know he was studying to be a doctor. There was a lot I was unaware of; admittedly I hadn't done my homework. Hell, I was a rookie. Decisions of this caliber were new to me. All I know is that it's easy to pull a trigger. People make a fuss about it. They talk about conscience and sweating and fear of the Judgment Day. I felt none of those things.

I saw the man behind the grocery store. I'll just call him Paul. I think we're on a first-name basis now. He was walking out into the dumpster area, carrying a large cardboard box. Apparently he and his family were facing an imminent out-of-state move and he was looking for packing material.

It was easy. I fired from the woods, and there was no one to witness what I did. Raise the gun, squeeze the trigger, retreat. I even took a moment to relish it before ducking out. The sound reverberated off of the brick wall. The wall was painted yellow, just like all back walls of all grocery stores across this great nation. I was surprised at how easily the shot came off. I found out later it had only been beginner's luck.

One small section of the wall now carried an orange hue. It was a mix of blood and paint, and it shined in the afternoon sun. Ha, ha, that inspired me with a new game of stealth: Paint Paul. O.K., that's not funny either. Go ahead and laugh at me. It's easy when you're over there, away from my gun.

He was my first. It would only get easier.

I heard the shot, enjoyed the moment, and escaped into the foliage. Paul was just practice, really. The Earth can spare a mulligan, I'm sure. I once saw a graph of human population over time. It looks like any other exponential curve you ever seen. With one exception. There was one genuine decline in the otherwise flat-then-spike-upwards nature of the graph. It occurred a few centuries ago, and you know it as the plague. Surely the work of the devil in the minds of those alive at the time, today it seems more like God's own hands in action. If you imagine the numbers on this good Earth had that not happened...well, Good Missus Nature would have no need for me now. Humans would have been downsized by this time, and maybe the world would be a better place because of it.

I expected to hear about Cristen's death by now. There had been no news. Perhaps she hadn't yet been discovered in all her glory, or perhaps the news was not grand enough to find its way onto the evening report. After all, she was an unmarried, childless woman who died with no life insurance, no controversial will.

In this society, that's one step above "Lost Pet" in terms of newsworthiness. Still, I had expected something, especially being that her "murder" occurred on the site of a vacation getaway. The more I considered that fact, the more assured I felt her death remained unknown to the world. I suddenly felt the urge to call my answering machine. I headed out of the woods, facial hair coming in well, and found myself a pay phone—not an easy task in today's wireless world, I assure you.

There were three messages. Three more than usual. It's that dreaded, steady, red light that loves to mock the lonely. One of the messages was a wrong number. Some lady named Judith was asking Frank what he wanted for dinner. My guess is that he was disappointed. She didn't sound like a very good cook, or a very good fuck for that matter.

The two others were from friends of Cristen's. They were unaware she and I had left together to camp, but called me knowing that I spent a lot of time with Miss Powers. I was her *boyfriend*. We all need labels, don't we? They make us feel so secure. Well, you're an *asshole*. Feel secure in that.

It wouldn't have bothered me if they had known I was with her at the time of her disappearance or even if they had known I killed her. After all, it was only a matter of time before my cover was blown. A part of me waited this moment impatiently. Once the chance of escaping unscathed was gone, there would be no going back. I would be committed to the task.

At last, the messages.

Tom Chambers: *Hey, Ed, it's Tommy. I was hoping you might know where Cristen's at. She was supposed to come over Friday. I'm sure she's fine. Probably just hangin' with you. Have her give me a call, will ya? Thanks, man. Hey, how about racquetball this weekend? Let me know.*

That punk would never play ball with the likes of me. He was just being polite.

Crystal Demora: *Edward, you know where Crissy's at? Pick up if you're there, huh? Let me know. Hope you're all okay. Ciao.*

I was always Edward, no matter how many times I objected to it. Only certain people—special people—may call me Edward.

"No more messages." That cold, monotone voice did its deed, announcing the fact that nobody else loved me. Nobody else loved me. Nobody loved me. I had... eliminated the one person who had shown a sincere

love for me since Jill. It hurt, I admit it, but I was sure of myself. I was working for the side of good, finally.

So, news of Cristen's death took a while. Actually, that's not even quite accurate. I never did hear of her death through my limited media resources. I hadn't seen a newspaper in a while, and television seemed like a distant dream. I heard murmuring in a town bar one evening, when I traveled in for supplies and foodstuff. Just the usual, "Can you believe something like this could happen so close to home?" kind of stuff.

Eventually Cristen's friends caught on, I'm sure, making the connection between her disappearance and my own. No doubt they first figured my body would turn up sooner or later, too, but even more surely, they figured me as the "killer" when it didn't. Not that they had reason to imagine me bringing harm to Cristen, but any time there's a man and a woman, the guy has to be doing something wrong, and nobody ever seems to be very surprised when that turns out to be the case. Bitches.

I have to imagine they were shocked by the realization that I might be involved in foul play. I'm not handsome, but I do possess a good deal of natural charm. I wish now that I could be alone in a room with them for ten minutes or so. I'd like to explain my true motivating force.

Cristen had fine friends, and I must admit I felt a loss when I was no longer able to hang out with them. Some of my finer memories in this lifetime revolve around board games and barbecues with those very people. Polite but bold, intelligent but humble, these were people I could relate to. Damn fate. Why do I have to be the one to save the world? I write this with only the smallest dose of angst.

The nature of people is in constant flux. Often we are hit with conflicting or even ironic emotions. This has no real surprise value when we strip away our theological ideals and realize that we are chemically powered beings caught up in a power struggle that doesn't care about the individual.

Biology is at first glance a communist state, with each of us receiving essentially the same tools to work with at birth: a brain, reproductive organs and opposable thumbs. Beyond that, though, the comparison is lacking. Perhaps it can only be thought of as carefully outlined anarchy. One bad gene and you pay the morgue an early visit.

It's this factor of the unknown that worries us all and leads to the kazillion-dollar antidepressant drug industry. And just as a society is always conflicted, so is the individual soul. Should I or shouldn't I? Does he or doesn't he? Our entire life is one big decision, hopefully under our own control but probably not.

It was because of this indecision and fear that it took me a while to get into the swing of things. I felt guilt at times, though I hate to admit that. What if I was wrong? What if I was wrong either in fact or in method? In the end, though, I figured I had started and I might as well finish at this point. The gun had sounded, and the horses were out of the gate. I might as well see if I could reach the winner's circle.

My second act in the name of God was even easier than the first, at least from a mental standpoint. Well, that's a lie, but I feel right saying it. Anyway, I feel compelled to make a clarification at this point. I use the word "God" because that is the word we are taught in this society. It is an acceptable way to express the greatest power in the Universe. Also, being only three letters in length, it makes for very efficient writing. Chances are, though, that you and I envision a very different God. My God doesn't hear my prayers. My God doesn't appear in doughnut frosting. My God is an energy, not a being. I use the term only because it is all to which you can relate. You limit me. Truly.

Actually, to speak the truth, you limit me in a number of ways. The English language—my archenemy— is one particularly nasty nemesis. There sometimes are not enough words. I might be able to express myself to one person one way, while someone else would have no idea what I'm talking about. Humans are stupid folk. When you hear someone speak a language that is foreign to you, you realize the truth in this. Suddenly we're just creatures who grunt to communicate, no better off than sea lions. Perhaps that's why we're all so defensive about our own language. A new, common language would be sobering and robotic, and this scares us. Otherwise, a lingua franca would have been established long, long ago.

Chapter Nineteen

(diecinueve, dix-neuf, diciannove)

I did take a lesson from my second act. Actually, come to think of it, I took two. It happened in the parking lot of a mall. Malls, the Serengeti of modern life, where people show off their money like sharpened claws and large, shiny fangs. We crowd to them, as we do to bars and beaches. These places exist for the show-biz atmosphere, which is reason one why you're not likely to meet your undying love there. I recommend stationery stores myself.

Tanned, muscular bodies and a legion of credit cards are our urine, which we expose to the world to mark our territory. Money is the modern piss. It grants us an advantage over the competition. If you can't outrun the horse, shoot it. And curse while you're doing it. People respect volume and vulgarity in this world, whether they admit it or not. "That guy's a moron" just doesn't work as well as "That guy's a fucking moron." Makes no sense, but it's true. We're well-trained.

It was now a half-hour before close. I took refuge behind an old, red sedan with worn seats and a bumper riddled with stickers displaying the logos of all the big rock-and-roll bands. A woman came out of the rear exit. The door was unmarked and was located beside a dumpster. I can only imagine that it was for employee use only. I stood in the fading sun for two hours, watching and waiting eagerly for the right person to walk out—the right feeling to hit me.

At last an elderly woman exited the building. She was wearing faux fur coat, which might actually be worse than the real thing. If you're going to make a statement, make a fucking statement. All this said was, "I can't afford the real thing." Her hair was white at the edges, and even from a distance, I could make out the deep lines on her face, which are a telltale sign of a rough-and-tumble life. She might have been sixty-five.

I wondered if someone would come by to pick her up. If she had left the area quickly, I might never have the chance to do my duty. But she didn't.

Instead she waited and smoked a lot of cigarettes. It grew dark, and dozens of other people happened by, exchanging hellos and good-byes. It seemed like fate. If I hadn't taken action at last, she might still be standing there, wasting virgin air and valuable real estate. I cocked my gun at 9:45 pm. I lifted my weapon to my shoulder and took aim.

I'm not a good shot. I would have made a terrible hit man. I had never shot a gun prior to my rendezvous with Paul, and I hadn't practiced since that time. I suppose I assumed it would come natural to a predator. After all, a shark isn't taught how to act in a frenzy; it goes on instinct. A protective layer glides over its eyeballs, and its jaws open indiscriminately to feed on anything that gets in its way, even if that should be a fellow shark, or its own tail.

I was wrong.

The bullet went astray and struck the woman in the shoulder. She went down, screaming. This time people *did* respond. I had to shoot again; I knew it. I couldn't let her survive. Not because I feared capture, but because I feared failure. I squeezed the trigger slowly with my index finger. This time my aim was true, and the bullet struck her squarely in the temple. It was a messy sight. A group of horrified onlookers turned in my direction and stared directly into my eyes before taking shelter themselves. I was sure the woman would die, if she hadn't already, but I was even more sure my anonymity was a thing of the past. Now it was *serious*.

I ran down an embankment into the wooded area across the street and began to strip. I'm not sure why I did this. I can only figure, in retrospect, that I subconsciously believed I would shed both my guilt and my chance at capture along with my wears. In the end, I wore only a T-shirt, jeans, and my boots. My boots were sturdy, rugged and old. I had now owned them for two years, wearing them most of those days. I would not have traded them for two bricks of solid gold.

Gone behind me were the button-down, the hat, and the sunglasses. Maybe I left more evidence at the scene, but personally, it felt like salvation. It was like a cleansing process, a baptism into a new faith. I had not been baptized. It felt fresh and affirming. I was at last announcing my presence in the world *to* the world. It was time to accept responsibility for all of my actions and to act upon my beliefs. I was ready to meet my fate head-on. Thank God for the small boy who taught me everything. I'm sure you know him, if you think about it hard enough, you leper head.

But then again, what do you know?

Chapter Twenty

I told you that I learned two lessons from the event. This is true.

The shooting, or rather my lack of marksmanship, had created a messy scene. I felt like I was dishonoring nature by using such an amateur method of creation. By creation, I mean that I was creating opportunity for fresh, new life in the natural world by eliminating parasites from its premises. It's much like thinning the forest canopy or setting controlled fires on the savanna to allow for new growth.

The blood also shocked me. It all felt a little too real. It's hard to deny your human feelings. After I found a place deep in the woods, where I was sure of my privacy, I vomited repeatedly. I hadn't planned on this, and was disappointed in my own lack of discipline. I decided then and there that a new means of completing my mission would have to be sought. The thing is, I always came back to the gun in the end. Efficiency is a priority when it's you against the world.

Secondly, I realized I had made a terrific error in my choice of the old woman. She was long past the hot flashes of menopause. That well had run dry twenty years ago. She probably didn't possess even half of her original teeth. She no longer could contribute to the gene pool and was an ineffective inhabitant. My effort had accomplished nothing except to provide work for the medical examiner.

I realized then I would need to make better decisions in the future. It was my obligation to do so. I should look for the foul, the diseased, the decrepit-minded, sure, but they must also have the ability to pass these nasty genes to future generations. After all, nature herself would have taken the old lady from us before too long; it didn't need my help in that.

Chapter Twenty-One

During the next year, I took out five bad seeds—two women and three men. They were high-strung for glory and self-fulfillment, the pettiest of ideals. This is the world of the *us,* not of the *me.* I hadn't had the best life, but I still made the decision to put my place in the world before my own selfish desires. My wishes are temporary and changing. The needs of the world at large are profound and righteous. If I, a weak and modest man, could prioritize correctly, why couldn't they? Their jobs, their class status and all sorts of other demographics varied immensely. I was not discriminating.

Each job was easier than the last. I rethought my method, though I eventually changed nothing in this regard. Like I said, I always came back to the gun. What changed was my attitude, my resolve. I achieved an inner peace that no high-tech electronic gizmo could provide me, and I swear I never felt an ounce of guilt or regret after the woman at the mall. Twelve months later, though, I was left wondering about the next step. I felt I wasn't doing enough.

By this time, I was far away from that mall. My work started to catch up to me, and I was forced to take on a disguise. What irony. We make the righteous hide out, while the demons among us are free to spread their psychological larceny. The bad people—an out and out minority, remember—are allowed to continue in their heathen style because the rest of us are too afraid to speak out. We fear what it will mean to us if we go against the grain.

Each of us shakes our head in private when we dwell upon the acts of the criminal mind, but in public, we wax stoic and act out for the cause of indifference. In the end, we are all grown up high-schoolers who want to look cool in front of our spouses, our parents, our children. We look to the corrupt and the greedy as we did to our first cigarette, as something new and exciting and elicit, as something to wake the beast within us that was put to sleep so long ago by the forces of monotony and dispassion.

I'm not sure what would have happened if my life continued on that track. I probably would have no real lasting impact on the world. On Judgment Day, I probably would have been meek, knowing I had been afforded all the weapons and yet had failed in my one reason for being. All I would have to cling to was the fact that I had found true love. Jill would have stolen my thunder yet again. Then I met Darien Kuff.

My friend.

Chapter Twenty-Two

She, too, was modest in look. I began to wonder if it might be a part of the deal. No need to give the gorgeous any more power. I first encountered Darien in a dive bar in Atsboro. I suppose it was no coincidence that we were both there. Places of solitude and refuge were becoming harder to locate. Here, among the dirt and the dinge, I was assured that few of my fellow drinkers had shining records. They, too, were probably avoiding attention. D.K., as I like to refer to her from time to time, approached me as I drank a martini. I had adopted these gin drinks like a new son. They did well for me and cleared out the cobwebs of my past. It was 10:30 pm.

She approached me when my drink was empty and mentioned that she was ready for a refill. I took the hint and signaled to the bartender for another round. He nodded and began mixing our elixirs. Conversation started with pet peeves. The misuse of the word "literally" was one of hers. She also didn't like pencil tapping, too much makeup, and people who wear corduroy. I'm not sure if she was serious about that last item; it might have been her attempt at humor. She was cool, but not especially funny. I mentioned pretense, people who leash their cats, and those selfish people who take their sweet time at the green arrow, knowing *they'll* make it through the intersection for sure. It was light talk (ha-ha), to be sure, but I didn't mind.

I studied the look of my new companion. She was about 5'7", as I had seen when she approached me, but she appeared much shorter when seated due to a tendency to slouch. Her hair was a strange gray-brown, and she appeared to be about five years older than I was. She was curvy, but I was sure her curves had been better placed in her twenties. Everything seemed out of place and slanted. It was nice to sit with a woman who didn't intimidate me with her looks.

She wore faded jeans and a green top, and

smoked ceaselessly, as was revealed by the premature deep grooves in the skin on her face. There was one redeeming quality to her outward appearance. She had a sprite-like, impish smile, with one corner of her mouth upturned and quite a few teeth exposed. The best word I can think of to describe it is devilish, although even that doesn't do it justice.

I asked her what she did for a living, and she explained that she was a painter. I found this a bit surprising, for I didn't figure there to be too many female painters out there, although it is a changing world. I've been told that I have a streak of misogyny in me, and I suppose at times I do condescend, but really I just think that men and women have a place in the world. Women in the kitchen, and men...nah, I'm just kidding. I won't even go there. Too many angry bitches out there.

Upon seeing the puzzled look upon my face, she explained that she was not a house painter, but an artist. I had to smile wryly at the fact that she indeed did not paint houses. Somehow, I felt validated, although I suppose that's sad.

Darien traveled to various small towns and created old-fashioned quaint paintings of barns, farmland, and the like. She didn't work for anyone specifically. Rather, she freelanced her work out and sold by word of mouth and advertising. Beyond this, the details of her explanation become fuzzy. I must admit I was not fascinated by the conversation. She must have noticed this, because she trailed off mid-sentence at one point. She stopped, took a sip from her drink, and checked her watch. She looked up again and studied my face, looking for something. I could almost see the wheels spinning inside her head, and I wondered if she would ever speak again. For a moment, I thought she was going to reprimand me for being a poor listener, and I felt a little sweat on my temple. I am not good with confrontation, especially when it occurs in public. Finally she spoke.

"So how does it feel to be in your position?"

The question intrigued me, because I hadn't even mentioned my endeavors in advertising. "Advertising has been good to me, and it allows the creative juices to..."

"That's not what I meant."

She took another sip from her vodka tonic, a much larger sip than the last. Then she lit up a cigarette. She removed another from the pack, which sat nearly crumpled upon the bar in front of us. She used the first cigarette to light the second, and then motioned for me to take it from her. I obliged.

"I'm not sure I know what you mean."

"What I mean is, how does it feel to be one of us?"

The sweat on my temple reappeared, and I inhaled deeply of the smoke in my left hand. The bar was dark, and the cherry glowed brightly. Cigarette cherries are like the glow from underneath the copy machine's cover—eerie and alien.

"One of..." I trailed off, believing I must be mistaken in her intent.

"Oh, come now, Ed. One of the chosen."

"I'm afraid I don't know what you mean."

"Sure you do. Does it feel good to do your job? Does it feel righteous to kill and to preserve? Each one is better than the last, isn't it?"

I was panicking, wondering if perhaps I was talking to a police officer. Was she trying to entrap me? How much did she know? She seemed to sense my anxiety.

"It's O.K., Ed. I'm one of us too. I know about Cristen and... the others. I know all about you. I might even know you better than *you* know you."

"But how...how do you know?"

"You develop a sense when you've been in the business as long as I have. I suppose whoever's steering the ship allows us one refuge—each other. Soon, you too will be able to pick up on it."

"But how do you know so much about me?"

"Oh, I know more about you than just the people you've killed." She said this a bit too loudly for my tastes. I put a finger to my lips and shushed her.

"It's O.K., Ed. I could scream it to the rafters if I so desired. People might listen, but they can't hear.

They are too self-absorbed. They are only half lives." She paused. "Oh, you have so much to learn. Even if they did hear, you'd be in no danger. There would be no proof."

"Of course there would. There are the weap— the implements, and there's DNA and..."

"No, there isn't. Do you really think it's all that simple? Do you really think of yourself as a simple spoke in a wheel? Do you still think of yourself as a man? Because you lost all that a long time ago—the day you sent Cristen up the river, in fact."

I smirked at the near literalness of her statement. "What else do you know?"

Her drink was empty, and this time she signaled for a refill. Then she looked at me, and I took the hint yet again. I reached for a ten dollar bill in my pocket. Clearly, bribery exists in all worlds at all levels.

"I know about Jill and that awful man. In a way, you should be thanking him though."

"Excuse me?" I felt as though I had just been punched.

"If he hadn't done what he did, you'd still be a hot commodity as a husband, and eventually a father. You would have made a terrific mainstreamer."

I later learned that this is the technical term for what I had referred to up to that point as 98-percenters.

"The gift would have been saved for someone less qualified for the other realm—our realm. You would never have lost your mortality or gained a greater sense of the world. You have a new perspective now, Edward. You're seeing the band from backstage. You're playing with fire, and you can't get burned. It's a terrific responsibility, but also a very special blessing."

"Why us?"

The bartender—a burly man wearing a flannel shirt—set Darien's drink in front of her. The glass was sweating.

"You've always felt a bit out of place, haven't you?"

"Sure. Always."

"There's a reason for that. You have insight. You can see and feel things about the world that other people could never imagine, or, more accurately, could never be bothered with. You have a sense about other people that is exceedingly rare. Do you think it was merely your good fortune that the only two women you ever approached happened to be such uniquely loving individuals? Are you really that naive?"

I readjusted my ass in my seat, suddenly feeling better about myself. I hoped that it was justified.

"Nature logs people like you—like us. It marks you from birth and follows you. From the small group of people who are prepared for the task—perhaps 5% of the population—nature chooses those who wind up in the best position for such authority. When Jill died, well, it was only natural for you to be promoted."

"You speak of the natural world as if it's alive and planning. How does it know? How does all this occur?"

"I don't have all of the answers, Ed. If I did, I'd be in charge, and not sitting here talking with some shlub at a dive bar."

"How long have you been...in the business?"

"Since I was fifteen." I was shocked to hear this, but I wasn't sure why. Perhaps I figured this to be a new phenomenon, as if the world had only started performing its tricks upon my birth.

"My God, how many people have you...?"

"Hundreds. I stopped counting a long time ago. It no longer matters. There's no quota to it, but you'll develop a sense of what needs to be done and when to do it, if you haven't already."

"And how many of us have you met?"

"Hundreds. You can do the math, though. At one percent of the population, I've had to go through a lot of people to meet so many. At least in the beginning. After a while, your senses fine-tune and you can weed out the mainstreamers much more quickly. Also, you meet people through people. It's not all that different from 'real life' in that regard. Finally, there's a trick to it...to sensing the one-percenters."

I was finding it difficult to get past the fact that she had started at fifteen, and yet again, Darien seemed to sense what I was thinking.

"I was young, yes. And it was difficult when I

first began to get the sensations. You think adolescence is difficult under normal circumstances. Ha! What's acne in comparison with being a mercenary for the gods?"

"What about your parents?"

"No. It's not hereditary."

This seemed strange to me, since the entire process revolves around genetics.

"I hid it at first, but this became increasingly difficult. While people are pretty out of touch for the most part, mothers are mothers, and I knew she'd figure something was up eventually. So I left the house when I was seventeen, and I haven't seen or spoken with my family since that time."

"Holy shit."

"It was a sacrifice, sure. But I realized I now had a more important authority to answer to. Parents just provide the organs to get you into this world. Really, they don't have much importance beyond that. Frankly, I'm surprised at how much importance your world places on family—relationships not of your choosing."

"*My* world?"

"Oh, sorry. Bit of a Freudian slip, I'm afraid. After a while, you'll be able to separate your past life from your current life, and this will no longer be your world. You'll be ethereal. But for now, you're a newbie. You're still straddling the fence, sorry to say. I would work on objectivity if I were you; you'll need it in this business."

I stood up, taking a sip from my drink. I really needed to downshift to beer. I got the flannelled bartender's attention, ordered a pint, and excused myself to the men's room.

I entered the restroom and checked myself out in the mirror. I looked tired and road-worn. I wondered how I would ever survive another year of this, always on the run and bearing some measure of guilt, even if I tried to deny it. The fluorescent lights hummed eerily, and I walked to the toilets. I really had to dig around to find my prick. The alcohol and the stress had shriveled it, and I found myself having to stand very close to the lip of the urinal in order to pee. How could such a majestic organ crawl into a figurative cave when things started to get hot? Jill had loved that particular part of me, and our sex life had been fantastic. We did it everywhere, every way. I think the fact that we were both young at heart (read: silly) helped our love life. We were always willing to try something new.

I finished peeing and took a last cursory glance at the mirror over the shoulder while I flushed my urine into the netherworld. My piss had been clear. I needed to cut down on the alcohol.

I exited the restroom to reclaim my seat next to Darien, who was still slouching and still smoking.

I took the empty seat and reached for my beer. I paused a minute to contemplate my next question. I felt I had to take advantage of this wellspring while I had it available to me. Finally I said, "Who was your first?"

She turned to me with an angry, perplexed look in her eyes. "Excuse me?"

"When you were fifteen. Who was it?"

Darien stood up, grabbing her purse.

"Who the hell are you to ask me that?" Her tone was stern, and her voice loud. Her voice was different somehow. Others at the bar turned to see what was happening.

I felt very uncomfortable. "Darien, I didn't mean anything by it. I'm just trying to learn."

Darien turned to the bar. "Jim." She called to the bartender, who then took leave from his place beside the register. He approached me.

"Excuse me, is there a problem?"

"No, sir, I was just asking a question."

"Jim, he was asking me about my first. I don't really think that's any of his business."

Jim nodded at her, and turned to me again.

"Listen, buddy, I think it's time you found your way out of here. It's four dollars for the beer."

"Darien, why are you doing this? You're one of us." Now she was red-faced.

"I don't know you; please leave me alone. I don't appreciate this at all."

Jim was looking at me angrily. The other patrons were looking at me angrily. It appeared Darien was a regular here, and well-liked. I suddenly felt that I should leave. I headed toward the door, and as I neared it, I heard something I'll never forget. It was Jim's voice.

"I'm sorry, Shirl; I don't know where these people come from. Next one's on the house."

Chapter Twenty-Three

I ran out into the parking lot and crossed the roadway. I took refuge in the wood, the only place, it seemed, that I could find peace in my new life.

Had I imagined the whole conversation? Did the alcohol have such an effect? Was it nature's way of providing me with the information I so desperately desired? Or was she lying, simply divulging information and then taking cover behind her real-world guise? How could that be? The others at the bar would have seen me speaking with her earlier. It was important to me to find the answers to these questions, but I felt sure that I never would.

I felt very alone in the world at that moment, more alone than I ever had before. I spent the night huddled at the base of a tree in that forest, looking up through the canopy of leaves at the dark sky. The almost-full moon caused me to contemplate the state of life; we're all put here knowing nothing and we all leave here virtually the same way. It occurred to me that at that moment, there were thousands of other people in our hemisphere looking up at the very same moon, but I felt sure that none of them felt what I was feeling. I felt sure that none of them *could* feel this way. I felt both very powerful and very naive. That was the worst night I had ever experienced.

I awoke unrefreshed to the sound of squawking. The night air chilled me, and my back was damp from the forest floor. Looking at my surroundings, I tried to keep my mind on the serenity of the morning, but I found that I could not. Were the events of last night an anomaly? Had someone slipped me a pill? No, of course not. I was becoming paranoid; it's almost impossible to avoid when you're on the lam. I had kept on the move in the last year. I had spread out my work. This is the only explanation I can provide for my continued freedom.

Perhaps Darien was right, and nature did indeed provide me some degree of immunity. Certainly, without it I would have been taken in by now. Even living in the woods and cutting off all social ties—not an easy task, I assure you—I was still defying the odds by maintaining my independence. I limited my contact with reality as much as possible, gaining food from fishing and theft. I was careful. It would be all too ironic if I should get away with "murder" only to be taken in for petty theft. The jig would be up then. I took my food from private residences, mostly, away from the security cameras and prying eyes.

My mind came back to Darien. Was she—or at least my perception of her—an apparition, or would I meet more of these helpful but elusive souls? Would they continue to seek me out? I found that my eyes were beginning to tear, and I tried to fight off the emotion. I punched the tree under which I had slept. All this gained me was a pair of bloody knuckles. The year had passed quickly. I was alone and impassioned with a mission that was more important than I was.

Now, however, it was beginning to catch up to me. I feared imprisonment, I felt guilt, and I was lonely. I had never been a people-person. Indeed, for the first nine months, I had enjoyed my forced super-independence. The grim reality was settling in that we are social creatures, even the freaks among us. I missed camaraderie, and I missed *women*. Physical affection and attention was becoming a priority. I decided that something needed to be done.

I spent the day working my way eastward. At first I was on foot, but I borrowed a bicycle from a rack outside the library's entrance. The risk was minimal, as there was no one in sight and I'd be a mile away in minutes. There wasn't much to the decision process.

I rode for the better part of four hours until I hit a decent-sized town. I can't remember the name of the city now; details are becoming harder to recall. I stopped at a diner and asked a waitress if I could borrow a phone book. I was careful to keep a low profile. It suddenly occurred to me that I had absolutely no idea how one secures a call girl or how much their services cost. I had always seen those escort services listed by the dozens in the big cities. I assumed the process was one of picking and choosing. They probably wouldn't have much of a rooting out process. I mean, how much power could you command if you had to sink to fucking in back alleys to make money? Just enough to get a-hold of some crack, I guess. Okay, that's a stereotype. Forgive me, I'm just an angry man I guess.

This was no big city, though. It isn't exactly as though there is someone you can go to for advice in such a situation. I became angry and walked out of the diner, forced to spend another day alone. My gift was quickly becoming my burden. I felt anger towards the world for first providing me so little common sense in a society where it is crucial and then putting such a responsibility on my shoulders. I began to think it might be easier just to give up on life, but I had failed before at such a goal, and I was certain that I would fail again should I try. If Jill's death hadn't been enough inspiration, a little loneliness certainly wouldn't do. I never even put the gun's barrel to my head.

Most of us are born with a dual link to our world: Mom and Dad. They ground us; give us a starting point, a meaning. Those of us who are lucky find them to be a source of love and inspiration as well. From them we find purpose: to go forth, aim for success—whatever that means—breed, and die. Along the way we encounter fortune and famine, and gather resources which hopefully enable us make some sort of sense of our surroundings.

Sure, there is help along the way, in friends for instance. Perhaps a handful of people can be counted upon for guidance and support, with the rest serving as drinking buddies and golf partners but never really forging a heartfelt relationship. We might find reassurance in pets, in our work, in the attitudes of those around us. Often we do not. On the days when it is cloudy, when our bus is late, when our stomachs are queasy, we feel as though it will never get better. Soon, though, we find renewed solace from whatever escapes we have chosen for ourselves.

In the end, our parents typically have the largest role in our lives. When we lose them, we suddenly feel lost and very, very naive. The world is very large, and we are very small. Our link to the past is gone, and this frightens us to the bone. We look around and see myriad dangers over the horizon. If we are old enough and established enough, we persevere. It is not so easy on the young. Orphanages across the land house numerous people who have an uphill battle in front of them. Yes, the loss of one's parents is extreme.

Imagine losing an entire society—a culture—and you get some sense of what it feels like to be on the run. There is nowhere to run, no one in whom to take solace. Some forge new identities and hide within the false shelter it creates for them. Me? I never had a shelter to begin with. I was a natural pariah who, due to circumstances not within my control, had now attained a new outcast status. I needed to channel my anger and frustration into my work and find some measure of success in it in order to regain a sense of pride and self. I decided I needed someone to share this feeling with. I could never replace Jill, for she was unmatched in this world. But I needed someone, and it would have to be soon.

As it turned out, it was the very next day.

Chapter Twenty-Four

I had visited museums frequently in my youth. I was especially fond of natural history museums and the fossil evidence they contain. I was interested in what scientists call biological parallelism—similar adaptation over time in different species. The forearm in primates, for example, is akin to the fins of a fish and the wings of a bird. At least I think that's right. I'm no scientist.

Anyway, I find this all rather dazzling. Two creatures, perhaps unrelated, adapting similar physical structures, modified or enhanced only in response to different physical pressures. To me, it implies a purpose, although the evolutionists out there insist there is no greater scheme. Bollix! That's just politics speaking. Life *is* purpose. The development of language, the response to new and different diseases, and the creation of new species—it's all rather tidy. Sometimes nature's adaptations can even provide a little comic relief. Need I mention flatulence? What would the world be without a cutting fart? No, there is a purpose that we cower from.

While I couldn't tell you what this purpose to life on Earth is, I knew that I had an active role in its progression, and that's more than most people can say. The only true control we have over our lives is awareness. I planned to make the best of my newfound awareness.

As I said, the next day I made a friend. It was Samantha James, the girl in the woods. I have told you our beginnings; I was in a rush to do so. I felt it was important. But our initial contact was now behind us.

Her eyes focused on me intently, as if studying me. I could see fear, but not terror. It was as though she were trying to hide her anxiety, as if I was a stray dog and could sense it if she showed a hint of despair. Oh, child, what have they taught you in this world of yours? Even now, I am forced to laugh.

I continued, since she seemed hesitant. Her

indecision was understandable, for she was new to this and I'd had a year to prepare for our rendezvous in the woods. Had it been a year already? It seemed like only yesterday that inspiration had struck me.

"Relax, I'm no stalker, no hell worm. I am just a man with a cause who needs someone to listen. It's hard finding someone to listen, wouldn't you agree? To really listen, I mean." Many people inject random "mm-hmms" and wait for their turn to speak. They never really listen.

After a few seconds elapsed, she nodded her head almost imperceptibly. I figured she was humoring me. I do not like to be humored.

"You were probably prom queen," I said. She looked up at me quizzically. Women often look at me quizzically, typically for the wrong reasons. I suppose I'm more of a figure of morbid curiosity than one of intrigue. Fair enough.

"Am I right? Prom queen?" I got no response. This cat-and-mousing was starting to irritate me.

"Come on, Sam. Tell me, were you prom queen? Belle of the ball? It is in your best interest to answer. Friendships are based on trust. You should know that."

"No." She shook her head slowly to reinforce the answer.

"Really? I'm surprised. Well, I'm sure you were a popular thing in school, nonetheless. I can't imagine why you might be cashiering, though. A girl like you, I figured someone to be looking after you, caring for you, providing for you." I looked at her hand; there was no ring. I didn't see Sam as the type to reject an old tradition, so I took her to be single.

"Sam, I don't ask that you speak much. I understand your situation here. Trust takes time. Perhaps later you will wish to contribute to the conversation. For now, I only ask you to listen. Would you care for a drink first?" I had a gallon jug of water with me, which I now lifted from the ground beside us. She glanced at the jug, and I could see from her first reaction that she was thirsty, dehydrated.

"No." There was a pause, then: "No, thank

you." Ahh, politeness. They are always polite, hoping to appease their captor. Hollywood doesn't lie. If only I could explain to her that I was not a kidnaper, that I was no shadowy figure who lurks in bushes behind college dormitories. Alas, I could not, and I suppose this is why she turned down the water she so clearly desired. I drank in large sips from the jug, not to make her envious, but to try to encourage her to do the same. Besides, I was thirsty too.

"All right, Sam. If you change your mind, let me know. We're in this thing together, you know, at least for a little while." The last of that sentence gave her a start. "No, Sam. I just meant..."

I trailed off, realizing that she wouldn't believe me anyway. No need to waste my breath on that. I had enough to say as it was.

"Sam, you seem like a bright girl. I'm sure you've heard of evolution." Of course she had, but like they say, even the longest journey...

At first there was no response, and I almost rolled right into my next sentence, willing to make the assumption. Finally, it seems, she surprised me with a little ribbing—probably just a defense mechanism. I could respect that.

"I'm Catholic," she said.

This time I took my time in replying.

"Oh, really, and a staunch Catholic at that, I am sure. Church every week and such. But I'll give you the benefit of the doubt. Am I correct to take your response to mean you don't believe in evolution?"

She didn't answer, probably afraid now of giving the wrong answer. I waited for a response.

"I don't know."

"You don't know, or you're afraid to answer? Because there is nothing to fear here, Sam, except ignorance." Again a wait. I touched her cheek, and she shied away from me. Exasperated by the circumstances, she replied at last.

"I...I believe."

"Good. That's settled, so we can move on." I sipped from my water bottle again, and made a gesture to offer her some, but she turned her shoulders away.

"Samantha, for a long time I wandered the Earth, just as you do, wondering what my purpose here is and how it managed to stealthily elude me. Certainly we can't all be here to drink beer, sell cars, and tattoo our asses." I paused to look at a chipmunk in the clearing. That small creature seemed at that moment to have plenty of purpose. Boy, those sons of bitches are as cute as buttons, ain't they? The sun was coming out, the rainwater on the leafy floor glistened, and all was right with the world. Moments such as that are rare in this life.

"Finally, following the death of someone I loved very dearly, I realized my purpose here." I noticed that I had put another start into my new friend. "I didn't kill her, Sam. She was taken from me by the vile filth of which I now rid the world, but that can wait a moment. Here, I insist." I held the jug of water to her lips, and at last she drank. Thirst won out in the end; it always does.

"I'll spare you the techno-talk; I'm not one for jargon. The essence of it all is that our genes are passed on in a wonderful process that, despite what you might hear, works toward a greater good. The problem, though, is that we've fouled up the works. Instead of taking nature for the generous mother she is, we've trashed her system.

Our technology and our greed are making evolution obsolete; the ill-minded and ill-bodied now survive. It's rather alarming. But the Earth is resilient, as you well know, Sam. People like me are put here to level the playing field. You see, I am but one of one percent of the population who have the enviable job of reestablishing natural force as *the* force to be reckoned with, as it should be. Do you understand?"

The look in her eyes screamed, "*Murderer.*" I was saddened by this. I had hoped for more. She was so young, I thought she might yet be unfazed by the garbage our heads are filled with by the media and others out for no damn good.

"Please, Sam, say something."

To my surprise and relief, her response was immediate.

"What do you want?"

"Aren't you listening?" It was an angry tone. I settled myself. "I want you to listen, and hopefully to accept. I am letting you in on the world's biggest secret. It took an unfortunate and untimely death to make me wake up. I am trying to save you the same pain. You see, we can help each other. You can lend me an unaffected ear, and I can teach you."

She had her head down.

"You are young and obviously bored with the world. I hoped—I still hope—that you will be open to new opportunity, to new ideas." My train of thought had been interrupted. I gathered myself. "Do you have a boyfriend, Samantha?" I sensed fear once again. "I ask you this only because I hope you have someone you can love as much as I loved my wife. Only through love are we able to see the world with passionate and curious eyes. We are inspired by one another."

"No. No boyfriend."

I doubted the validity of this statement, but gave her the benefit of the doubt.

"That's too bad. I'm sure you will find your happiness in time. Anyway, there is not much more to tell. I thought it would take forever to explain, but like anything else, when you weed out the extraneous crap, it's all fairly basic stuff. Good versus evil, just like in the movies. Now, I have told you so much about me, but true understanding is a two-way street."

She didn't take the hint, or at least she didn't lead on that way. I continued.

"What do you like to do?"

She didn't answer. I was prepared for it. I had been alone for most of a year. I could wait. "It's O.K. Take your time. I'm in no hurry. I stepped behind her to let nature work for *me* for a change. I urinated on the wet forest floor and felt great relief in my midsection. Steam wafted up from the ground, and a sweet smell found my nostrils.

"I like to bike ride and to read."

"Reading. Very good." I zipped up my fly and returned to my space in front of her. There was a mild burning in my abdomen. I continued:

"Yes, books are a very good start. We should remember, though, that they merely act as inspiration and guidance. It is easy to forget about the larger world beyond. What type do you read?"

She dug her foot into the soft ground. "Romance."

"Well, I must say, I am disappointed. A bright girl like you reading such trash. Besides, true romance awaits you in the real world. Why look to the uncaring pages of a book to find it?"

She must have taken the last to be rhetorical, so I repeated myself.

"Why look to the uncaring pages of a book to find it?"

"I like reading about it. It's...comforting."

"Ah, yes, it is, isn't it?" That one *was* rhetorical, and she took it as such. "What would you like to do with your life?" I took a cracker from my pocket and nibbled its edge. It was salty, and I spat it out onto the leaves below me.

"Teach."

"A very noble desire. Certainly it is. But what can we teach if we refuse to learn?" Admittedly, I was beginning to sound a little self-important, pretentious even. But it was my spotlight now, after all these years. I stifled a laugh.

"Kindergarten." This time I couldn't stifle. After all, we don't really teach kindergartners much of anything except how to share and get along. Come to think of it, maybe these are the most important things to know. I know more than one person who could use a refresher course.

"Very good, Sam, very good. Are you in college?"

"No."

"Why is that?"

"Money."

"Ah, yes, money. It all comes down to that, doesn't it? You need it to get it. Well, certainly you will find a way. A mind like yours should not be wasted. You are so bright... and beautiful. You remind me of someone I once knew." There was a long quiet.

Finally, she asked: "Your wife?"

"Hmm. That's very perceptive of you, and

also very presumptuous, but I give you full credit for listening. What is it you kids say? Props?" The sun was out in its full golden suit by now. "My Jill was both a beauty and a smart woman, I must admit. She had the double barrel effect going for her. A very rare creature. I'd give just about anything for five minutes with her. And do you know what I'd do with those minutes?"

"I can imagine." Apparently her fear was quelling. This was good. I wanted her to feel comfortable. Her eyes were still red, though. I knew that the fear still remained inside. She probably just didn't want to piss me off.

"You're wrong. I'd use my five minutes to thank her with every ounce of my being. She was my light. She was my fire. She was everything to me, more than I deserved. And some bastard took her from me. Do you know how that feels?"

"No."

"It's gut-wrenching. It tears your heart out."

"Why are you telling me this?" Her voice was still weak and fluttering. She hid her eyes from me when she spoke. I wished that I could have met her in a bar and had this conversation under different circumstances. I felt I could have loved her. I knew she would have loved me. My voice is soothing. I'm quite charismatic for someone so invisible.

"Because I needed to tell someone, and as I told you, you are young and innocent of the indifference that befalls us as we age."

I had smoked several cigarettes during the course of our discussion, and they were forming a pile in front of me. I am mildly obsessive compulsive. I like neat piles, straight lines. It is an affliction, and not one I'd wish upon anyone.

"I am afraid, Sam. Why, you ask?" I did not wait for her to ask; I knew she wouldn't.

"I am afraid because I am alone in the world. My father was in my life only for a short time. My mother no longer is. My wife died. My girlfriend died." I saw Sam react to this. "Again, not me. It was diabetes." I lied, yes, but only because she would never understand the truth. Too much too fast. "I am alone."

"We're all alone."

"What do you mean we are all alone? You're not alone. You have a family and friends and coworkers and..."

"We're all alone. Nobody knows why we're here, but we try to deal with it in...in other ways." I noticed that fear was turning to anger. I waved my gun by my side, for emphasis.

"In normal ways? Is that what you were going to say?" She looked away, afraid. "No, Sam, it's all right. I want the truth."

"In other ways."

For an instant, I had cracked her, and I was afraid now it would be the only time I would. She spoke again.

"What are you going to do to me?" The inevitable question. There was only one reply I could think of at the time.

"Nothing, Sam. Nothing."

But I knew that would not suffice. I wanted to kill her, thank her, mock her, and fuck her all at once. It was time to make a decision.

Chapter Twenty-Five

Isaw four options before me—actually three when you consider that I had already decided I must leave her alive. Her soul was intact. I could have her join me as an ally, but I couldn't foresee that being a successful endeavor. Even if I could trust her, Sam didn't have the makeup; she wasn't chosen for this type of life. Besides, at the moment it didn't seem that this would be *her* favorite choice. I could continue to hold her captive, taking her with me as I moved from place to place. I'd have somebody to talk to, who could live my adventure with me: a human log book.

This idea smelled of messy. There's the practical issue of keeping her hidden, not to mention having to supply food, water, etc. I couldn't see this as a fruitful decision either. This left me with but one option. I would have to take my chances and let her go. She had given me all I had wanted in the first place: an ear to listen. I had no reason to hurt such a delicate flower. She was on my side. Our side.

Rape never crossed my mind. Fucking, yes. Rape, no. But if we had fucked, it would have been rape, even if she pretended to enjoy it, out of fear. In fact, I'm a bit surprised I'm bringing it up even now. I was lonely and horny, not desperate for power. After all, I had more power than anyone in the world. I was a walking demigod.

"I'm going to let you go."

She looked at me hesitantly, not wanting to appear too excited, not wanting to get her hopes up.

"I told you I just needed someone to listen, and I meant what I said. I'm a man of my word. I'm not even going to give you the old shtick about not telling anyone. I can't imagine anyone keeping this experience to themselves, and nothing I can say now can keep you from going to the cops when you're out of harm's way. I can't just let you run free, though; I hope you can understand that. Just give me fifteen minutes. I slipped the bandanna back into her mouth, and laid a gentle kiss on her soft cheek. I whispered a sincere "Thank you" in her ear, and then I was off.

I walked across the street. I heard nothing from behind me. I was sure that Sam could get a scream past the rag between her lips, but she might be fearful that I was still around. Either way, I didn't want to dilly-dally.

I crossed the parking lot as nonchalantly as I could. I entered the five-and-dime next to the grocer and looked to buy a pen. Of course they don't sell them individually, so I was forced to buy a three-pack for $1.39. Considering that I only had about four dollars in loose change in my pocket, I had just spent about a third of my life savings on three black pens.

You see, I made a foolish move after Cristen's death. A wiser man would have stopped at the bank on the way out of the woods and made a withdrawal. Once I realized my error the next day, I was too afraid to visit the bank. I *had* been able to make several ATM withdrawals before my card was disabled. I'm still not sure how they got to me so quickly.

Regardless, that bank account had long been closed, and the 1,600 dollars I had withdrawn were spent. I suppose it was for the better. Material possession was now my enemy, though I sure wish I could have eaten better over the course of that year. I went hungry more than one night in that time.

You never realize what food means to you until you don't have it, and it's downright frightening when you don't. You keep looking at people who won't give you a handout as though they must be kidding. Certainly they wouldn't want to go hungry. I mean, what's a buck between two human beings? Then you realize that the cold reality is most people just don't care.

People just don't care. I suppose that must be what it feels like to go to prison. They put you behind those cold, hard bars and you look out at the guard, figuring it must all be a joke. "O.K., buddy, ha-ha. Now let me out of here. I've got laundry to do, and I have to mow the lawn." And the guard only stares back with a steely look in his tired eyes. I suppose it's only then that you realize the true meaning of independence. All those Fourths of July, I didn't even know what I celebrated. It was just a bunch of fireworks and rock music on the radio. A whole lot of hooting and hollering typical of empty American overindulgence. Hmm. Even with my anger, I never forget how many people have died for my freedom. Not anymore.

I exited the store minus $1.50 (tax), and walked to a green garbage receptacle, the kind which has the recycling symbol painted on its side. I reached inside, feeling around with intent. I was stabbed by something I thought was a needle. I remember thinking to myself what a dumb way to die: getting AIDS from a supermarket trash bin. But it was just a lollipop stick. Damn thing had a shard of candy left on the end of it. Finally my fishing hand hit pay dirt. I removed a newspaper in good condition. Looking inside it, I found a large coupon page that was nearly blank on the reverse side.

I used my recent purchase to scrawl a quick note, and then pocketed the pens. Who knows when I'd need them again. I pushed the edge of my letter into a crevice in the front panel of the soda machine, and I ran like heck's older brother, confident Sam would be released within minutes. Along with my explanation of where Sam was tied, I had written: "It is *you* who needs to be forgiven. May God have mercy on your soul." And I meant it. All except for the God part.

Chapter Twenty-Six

Itook to the woods again. Not only did the quiet, hidden shelter of the forest offer me a convenient hiding spot from the insanity beyond, it also made me feel closer to nature—my employer. The greenery of the tree leaves, the smell of the moss, the sounds of the birds—they all kept me focused and grounded. Just as an artist surrounds himself with color and beauty as inspiration, I had my own creative stimulation.

I retreated to the shadows as often as possible.

And so it was that later that afternoon I sat beneath a large tree, pondering the past and future. I needed to escape again. The trail was getting hotter faster with each event in my life. I found myself having to make decisions more quickly, with less and less time to react to new circumstances. As I sat under that tree considering my next move, I heard something from my left. It was footsteps.

I took my gun—Jill's gun—from my pocket, silently. I had come this far, and I wasn't ready to go down without a fight, even if it meant removing a healthy specimen from the gene pool. After all, I was more important than any mainstreamer. My life had meaning. I still had Jill to go home to.

I drew the gun in front of me. I could hear leaves swishing and twigs crackling as they broke beneath heavy shoes. Then I heard a voice:

"Ed... Edward Caine."

My hand clenched the trigger more tightly, and I came damn close to firing at nothing at all. Then it occurred to me that the voice was not totally unfamiliar. It was like a voice in a dream: fuzzy and muffled. Then I saw her.

She lacked both the physical presence of Jill and the spritely aura of Cristen. Her beauty was in her intellect, in her advanced knowledge of the world around us. I doubted the reality of her before me.

"Get away from me. I have a gun. You've done enough."

"Relax, Ed. The time was not right. You had taken enough from the lesson." Still, she might have been trying to trick me. She might be wired, or...

"Ed, it is time for us to move forward together... for Jill." Those words sealed it. It was Darien, and not "Shirl."

I'm not stupid. "Wait a minute. Stand right there." I still had my questions.

"If that was real—if *you* were real—how come those people at the bar didn't see us talking earlier that night? How come they were so quick to take your word?"

"You're not thinking, Ed. It was the nature of the situation. The folks there know me; you were a stranger. So I was given the benefit of the doubt from the start. Secondly, the woman is *always* given more credit. You should know that by now. Think about what I said. I didn't say I had never met you. I said I didn't *know* you. That's a truism, at least as far as they are aware. Certainly they don't know about all this nonsense. I tell them you're harassing me—a regular female customer—and they have you removed. Tits are a wonderful asset, no?"

"Wait a minute. How'd you even find me here?"

"You have a lot to learn, Ed. You are still limited because you don't think of yourself any differently. There is so much more to your role. Soon, you'll be able to find me anywhere I should choose to go, just as I found you. "

I was flipping through images of Big Brother in my mind, and she must have seen the grim look on my face.

"Feels a lot like you're being watched, hmm? Well, it's not like that at all. You're more free now than you ever have been. You'll see with time." She paused. I can only imagine she did so to take a breath, because her next thought was obviously as well thought out as those she had spoken thus far. I suppose she had given this speech about as often as Thelma Vicaro had given her own to my high school classmates.

"You want to know why I didn't tell you more. Why I had you kicked out. Well, I had to take care not to tell you too much too soon. I had to hold some cards back. These meetings tend to be overwhelming for newbies. I had to see how you'd react. Besides, you're much more likely to retain what I tell you this time around."

"I'd say I took it pretty well." I beamed.

"Oh, yeah. You were a rock, Ed. You kidnapped a girl. A young, virile girl at that. Like I said, you were a rock."

I was mildly insulted and wished to move this meeting forward as quickly as possible. I also remember thinking her method of handling the situation could use improvement.

"All right, Darien. So we've established you are who you say you are, and how you found me. What happens now?"

"Ed, that is for you to determine."

I hate responses like that. Talk about a pet peeve.

"Come on, Darien. That's bullshit. I'm feeling alone and unsure. You say I've got this great new responsibility, and thus far I haven't heard jack shit from anybody except you about what I'm supposed to do with it. Help me out here, for Christ's sake."

"Ed, you're not listening. When I said it's for you to determine, I meant it."

This time I didn't answer. Darien was smart; I knew that. I wanted to think about her intent. Closed mouth, open mind. She continued before I could come up with anything, however.

"Raise your gun, Ed."

I did, pointing it at a tree across a clearing.

"No. I mean, raise your gun at me." I did so, in Pavlovian fashion. Darien was the only one I knew who knew what I knew, if you follow. And she knew a whole lot more than me, I was sure. She spoke. I listened. I raised the gun to the level of her chest.

"Now fire." But I didn't.

I don't mean to contradict myself here. I just told you that when Darien spoke, I listened. This is true.

But pointing a gun and firing a gun are two different monsters. I wasn't ready to fire upon a... a being of her superior knowledge without a little chitchat first.

"Fire?"

"Yes, Ed. I want you to shoot me. Make me bleed."

"But why? Do you want to die?"

"No, Ed. I am long past that stage, although I am quite certain that you still consider the option from time to time. Here, give me the gun."

Things happened very quickly at that moment in time. She reached for my hand, which I pushed forward to make it easier for her to take the gun from my grip. I was very nonchalant, of course, not expecting any fast moves. Fast moves are what I got.

Darien grabbed my hand and laid her right thumb over my left index finger, which pressed up against the trigger. I never had a chance to react, and the gun went off while aimed directly at her chest. Darien fell backwards, and her dress rode up on her legs. Her shins were dirtied by the forest floor. The shot echoed throughout my surroundings.

She was down and quiet. I wondered what the hell had just happened. I was scared, again. Why had she done this? Why had she left me alone to fend for myself? Why hadn't she told me more? Most important to me, why had she laid this guilt upon me in my current state? These thoughts went through my head in a matter of seconds. I never even had a chance to move.

Then she moved.

And I jumped.

Chapter Twenty-Seven

"**Y**ou people really crack me up." She said this lightly, laughing as she did so.

I stood there, too startled to respond.

"You always need your explanations. I figured it would be faster this way, and by God, I was right. There's too much say in this world, and never enough do. It's so mortal of you, Ed; it's rather quite distasteful."

"You're alive, but how? Are you even bleeding?"

"Naw, nothing like that."

She spoke like a Texan who had just seen a cow. Entirely unimpressed.

"I took a little shake from the force. You can't stop physics entirely. But no blood, and certainly not death."

"You're immortal?"

I made the jump. *"I'm* immortal?"

"Nothin' of the sort. Slow down, killer."

I chuckled at the irony of her statement, as I was certainly nothing of the kind, at least in this instance.

"I'm immortal—to use your peasant word—to *you.*"

"I don't get it." I lit up a smoke. I took care *never* to run out of smokes. The stress relief was too valuable in my new world. If I could only thieve one item in a night, it'd be smokes. I'd rather go hungry till breakfast than be without them.

"Ed, we can't kill each other. Well, it is technically possible, but it would be a very difficult task, it would involve pregnancy, and you'll forgive me if I don't grant you the pertinent information at the current time."

She motioned for me to give her a cigarette. I was in no position to argue—a fact about which I am sure she was aware.

"It's kind of like a safety latch. If I could go 'round shooting all the one-percenters but me, there'd be too much power in too few hands."

"So it's like checks and balances."

"Now you're cooking with gas."

"What about... the other people? The mainstreamers? Are we immortal to them as well?"

"Absolutely not. A bullet from their gun would kill you as surely as one from yours would kill them."

"But the numbers..."

"Yup. There's a hell of a lot more thems than usses."

I pondered this for a moment. Then: "What if they revolted?"

She threw me a smile that made me feel very naive. "Revolted against a force they don't know about, let alone comprehend? Even if a few found out, the others would deem them crazy."

"And if the whole world found out all at once?"

"Well, I can't say for sure. I guess there'd be a whole lot of mutation going on. The world would change rapidly, and as far as I'm concerned, for the worse. I guess I can't answer that. There is one thing I can assure you, though."

I waited, knowing that there was no need to ask what the one thing was. Darien nee Shirl stubbed out her butt on the tree under which I'd been laying. She finished her cigarette in a few long draws, whereas I was only halfway through mine.. I suppose I hadn't been puffing away though, listening intently as I was.

"If *somehow* the naive, uneducated, overconfident species known as humans should *all* come to know about this phenomenon at once, well, I have every confidence that nature would respond, react, retaliate. It always has, son. It always will. You think you know a secret, do you? You think that what you and I are discussing right now is *news?* Shit, this wouldn't make the back page of the Universal Newsletter."

I almost stupidly asked if there was such a thing. Instead I asked, "How can you be so sure?" It was now my turn to put out my smoke. There was still a quarter-inch of tobaccky in there, but I was content.

"Honey, there is so much for you to learn. And one woman has only so much time."

"You're not gonna tell me you're actually 500

years old and shit like that, are you?"

"It only feels like it, Ed. It only feels like it."

I laughed. "Well, how is it that you can be sure?" All of this new information was both a relief and an emotional buzz. I didn't know how to react, and laughter seemed the most enjoyable option at the moment.

"I'm very tired, Ed. I have to move on."

"What? No way! You are not doing this to me again. What the hell am I supposed to do now?"

"Go fuck yourself." She said this as she walked away from me, both middle fingers pointed skyward.

This enigmatic woman was beginning to get on my nerves. I wanted to follow her, even to punch her, but I couldn't. I don't know why; I just couldn't. I just cried. She was like a wizard from the tales of fantasy I read as a youth. And now when it meant something, all her knowledge did me nothing. I shouted, "When will I see you? Will I meet others?" My mental paralysis was gone now, and all of my questions rose. "Can I bring back the good ones? Do I have any other influence on the world? Will I ever feel normal again?"

I was shouting to the air. She was gone.

Chapter Twenty-Eight

There are days when you question what the hell you are doing with your life. Those are special days.

Every day, we wonder about the little decisions we make: *Did I buy enough Italian bread? Should we take the minivan? Should I let Harry's mother take our bed, or should I insist she use the pullout couch?* These decisions, while having a definite effect on our daily lives, really are meaningless. Regardless of how we approached them, our general well-being would be unaffected and life overall would continue status quo. Then there are the special days. It is during these times that our mettle is tested. These are the decisions that form, shape, and determine our lives.

Now, don't get me wrong. Our lives are shaped by happenstance too: a freak lottery win, a car accident, etc. But as far as our control over our own destiny is concerned, some decisions far outweigh others. I can remember three such special days in my life. The first was the day Jill died. I wondered where I'd go from there. The second was when Cristen met her fate. I wondered where I'd go from there. The third and last was when I met Darien for the second time, in that forest. I wondered where I'd go from there. As so often happens, the decision was not made based on any occurrence; rather it was the result of a little thought and a lot of alcohol.

I got very drunk that night, and pondered my fate. As proof of my inebriation, I had a campfire lit. This is not typically the recommended course of action for on-the-run felons who are still at large in an area where they've committed some or all of their crimes. It was certainly a mean feat to start the fire in light of the recent rain, but I'm a trouper. I persevered and found wood that had been protected to some degree. Even so, my fire popped and crackled from the wetness of its fuel source.

I am a weak man. I knew it then, just as I

know it now. I had also been incredibly lucky to that point. Considering the magnitude of my crimes, it was shocking that there wasn't more pressure upon me. I suppose there are a lot of criminals out there. I imagined that the sporadic nature of my crimes and my constant moving didn't help the police any. After all, it's tough to track a murderer who has no motive *known* to mankind. Who the hell kills for the sake of genetics?

Nonetheless, I knew time was growing short. I couldn't depend on randomness to protect me for long. For all I knew, there could be a dozen officers staked out in the woods around me even as I sat beside my campfire polishing my gun. I could no longer settle for these haphazard one-hitter crimes. It was time to get serious.

Chapter Twenty-Nine

We rarely notice nature. Normally she's a light breeze off of the Atlantic or a rainy spring day that helps the flowers reach full color come summer. Once in a while, though, she gets really pissed. It's usually when she's been ignored. The Nor'easter from out of nowhere that piles literal feet of snow on unsuspecting mountain hamlets. The son-of-a-bitch hurricane that ravages the coast, leaving people homeless and helpless. The tornado winds that shoot cars off the road as though they were toys. Nature is both beast and bitch, and she's best left alone.

Now I was a part of Her. I was sure of this now. I was slowly losing my humanity and becoming part of a larger force. My soul was being enveloped, and not in the foul Madison Avenue way. It was as if I was plugged in to a new source of power. I had been given so much by Her that now I felt it was only right that I should represent Her as accurately and honorably as I could. As I said, it was time to get serious.

Suddenly, out there by the campfire, I wished for a better job. I'm not talking about higher paying or more creative or any of that Earthboy shit. Advertising had done well for me, as I've said. Besides, none of that mattered anymore. What I mean is, I wish I had held a job that provided me more...access to do as I felt right.

Nuclear physics would have done it. Or chemistry. I could poison a waterway. That would have been dandy. An engineering degree would have made for some very interesting, if time-consuming, possibilities. Unfortunately, it's hard to accomplish anything in the name of the natural world by coming up with creative catch phrases and drawing clever cartoons. Good copy doesn't exactly make anybody shit their pants or anything like that.

Still, I had to do something. The facts of my situation were sobering. No doubt I would soon be taken in and booked. Not long after that, I would be sentenced. It's not as though I had gone to great lengths to conceal my crimes or hide evidence. I had just taken care to run far and fast after each one. Well, until the latest rash, that is.

Yup, I'd be sentenced. The thing is, my crimes came in, well, unforgiving states. I was in the land of capital punishment, and there would be men out there who'd love to see my head fry like an egg.

I thought about that for a moment. I would be somebody's Jeffrey Simons. *Me!* Oh, if only they knew I was acting for good. Suddenly a terrifying thought entered my brain. What if Jeffrey... No, he couldn't be. I dismissed that thought. I dismissed it not because I knew the man was beneath the position. In fact, I know very little about his life before the murder spree, let alone about his skills and intellect. What convinced me that he was not a one-percenter was his victim: Jill. There was no explanation in the world which would convince me that her genes were bad.

Still, the thought lingered in my head.

Maybe he, Simons, wasn't a one-percenter. Let's assume that to be the truth. Is there any other reason, other than self-defense, that is a viable excuse for murder? Or for nine murders? Nine remorseless, cold-blooded murders? I was sure I couldn't think of one. But I felt differently still. What if I was missing something? What if there was something *I* couldn't comprehend? What if Simons was on a mission of his own? No, I decided.

He was nothing more than a creepy little twisted fellow who hadn't found his natural place in the world. Sometimes people are just plain mean. I concluded I had no reason to forgive Jeffrey Simons for what he had done to me, to us.

It wasn't an easy sleep for me, nonetheless.

Chapter Thirty

When I awoke, I felt listless. Whenever I felt badly, I tried to think of something funny. I thought, in this case, of the way old-timers refer to the turn of the century years as aught-one and aught-two. This one was always a rib-tickler for me, even before the hum and the buzz and the droning started. Even before I felt the calling the day I spilled the grape soda.

So what could I do? I hadn't access to large-scale weapons. I lacked the knowledge necessary for chemical play. How many options were left me?

Finally, I decided to do it in blue-collar fashion. I had tried to avoid such a situation; it's messy and dishonorable. But time was running short, and messy and dishonorable was still better than never happened at all.

I loaded my weapon, left the woods for what I imagined would be the last time, and headed out of town to the west, right along the roadway. I figured I'd let fate decide. If I were wrong in my decision, if I had somehow erred in all of my thoughts concerning life on this miserable rock, let me find out now. Let a police officer pull me over and throw me in the back of his cruiser with the siren blaring to announce my presence to the world—his world. Better yet, let some 16-wheeler slip on the pavement and crush me into a form unrecognizable to man. If I'm wrong, I want to know it. There's too much namby-pambiness in the world today. If I was a sinner, let the whole world cast me out at once in a loud, unfaltering voice. Grasp your stones and deliver them my way.

Once I get down that road unscathed, however, once I get down that road unscathed, fair warning to anyone or anything that crosses my path, for I would then be Master of my own domain.

Don't fuck with Mother Nature or her bitches.

Chapter Thirty-One

I t took me a long time to get to where I was going, which isn't surprising when you consider I didn't know where that was. I decided on the way to my fate I should take the opportunity to see and do the things I wanted. Fate owed me that, at the very least.

I pissed off of a high canyon bridge. That was fun. The urine traveled a long way down, and I certainly couldn't hear its splash through the surface of the water. As I was pissing, a bird flew overhead. I took my gun from my pocket and shot at the bird. I missed horribly. Apparently my aim hadn't improved much as I had thought. Then again, it's not easy to shoot with a dick in your hand. Birds: nature's little clay pigeons. Hey, maybe that's where they got that word. All right, I admit it... I'm a little slow.

After pissing off the bridge, I came to a small town with a lot of cops. I felt leery, so I stayed only long enough to buy some licorice. I always loved black licorice. I believe I'm in the minority, and I prefer it that way. Y'all can keep your cherry suckers and your pops. Anise is the way to go. It's a man's candy. After pissing off the bridge, I came to a small town—Ha!

Yup, I wrote that already. I just want to show you who has the power here. Don't you fucking forget that, slack jaw. And keep that fucking thermometer away from me. I don't need people like you going anywhere near my ears or my mouth or my ass. Who would *take* such a job? Medicine is so overrated. No, I don't like your type, Doctor; it is certain.

I am reminded, now that I think of it, that we often see the past through rosy spectacles, as if the world used to be perfect. The time between the flappers and the hippies. But that's just not true. The world was not always so kind to women, to foreigners, to gays. Maybe we're growing as a species.

Travel was not always so safe. Try crossing the states in a covered wagon, and your minivan will never seem so bad again. There were always wars and rebellions. There was always tragedy. The only difference is, now we hear about it all the time. All our goddamn technology keeps us informed. It brings us together, sure, but it also scares the crap out of us. The world has lost all of the mystery and intrigue of the past. So maybe it wasn't a better place back then, but it sure feels like it. Today's bad feels somehow worse.

Chapter Thirty-Two

I wanted to do something grand, even if it wasn't all technologically advanced and whatnot. I wanted to leave the media in a whirl of confusion, and maybe even shock some people. I wanted to teach the world a lesson. But the cops back there, they scared me. I'm not the type to get edgy, but they made me...leery. I was leery. I was afraid for my trigger finger. If I lost that, I'd have to find another way. It wasn't as if I was scared, mind you. I would have had the balls to pull it off any which way at this point. I wasn't some newbie anymore. I was Edward P. Caine, Renaissance Man.

It was a time of rebirth if there ever was such thing. A time when men's hearts were invested in the market and their souls were buried in the bottle. The Earth was dead in the new Millennium; that much is sure. So I wasn't afraid of doing it another way. But what other way was there? Poison was the only other way I knew, and I've already explained to you that I'm not a chemist. I'm tired of having to repeat myself, Jill.

My God, I hope she's looking down upon me now. I need all the help I can get.

I need a pill now. Sometimes they help, sometimes not. But they're the only friend I have in this world.

I took two. Just now. Real time, as the techno-geeks put it. What a bunch of horseshit.

I walked past a barn, an old textile mill, and several minor strip malls. I realized that as long as I waved this gun, wasn't nobody gonna push me off of the sidewalk. Maybe I couldn't walk down the center of the road, but the shoulder was mine. I stuck out my thumb, just to feel All-American. I didn't really want a ride, and I'm not sure what I would have said had someone stopped to offer me one.

Nobody stopped. I can't say I was surprised. And me being so pretty and all. Sometimes I like to stand in front of the mirror and stroke my hair, imagining myself as a pinup from the '50s. But don't go telling anyone that, or I'll blow your fucking skull apart.

Finally, after hours of walking, with the pissing bridge and the textile mill and the strip malls well behind me, I came upon a fabulous sight. There in front of me was a little beach. That might not even be the right word for it, actually. It was an inlet or one corner of a lake or something. Rocky sand led up to its shores, and it really wasn't much of anything at all. But you couldn't tell that by looking at the faces of the kids around it. Kids are precious, ain't they? They had a sparkle in their eye that day, as if this beach were all they cared about on the whole entire Earth. I wouldn't have blamed them if it was.

I suddenly realized I was receiving quite a few stares in my direction. It wasn't for my taut physique; that's for certain. Actually, I thought at first they must know my face from the evening news. For a moment I felt fear, which is ridiculous now that I think of it. After all, *I* had the gun. Who cared if they recognized me? Then I realized there would be no recognizing the clean-cut man in those photos on television. My clothing was ripped and my facial hair was unkempt. I looked rather like a bum, and come to think of it, I guess I *was* a bum.

Of course, to you that means I'm also unfit for living. Time to take the old dog out back and put it out of its misery. Pa, grab your rifle. It takes one fucked-up society to look at someone down on his luck and see a villain. One fucked-up society indeed. And I used to be one of you.

Yup, it really bothers me. I used to sidestep the panhandlers as though they were shit on the sidewalk. Those are days I am not proud of.

So I was taking their stares, and I didn't care. It was a beautiful blue-gelatin day, and the sand reflected the sunlight. The birds were chirping, the water lapping. A man with his nose painted white with sun block sold ice cream and frozen candy bars from an insulated chest.

There might have been fifty people there that day, about half of them under the age of twelve. There were a couple of old-timers, real grizzled-like. There were also some teenagers necking and jostling for blanket room. The adults scoffed at them, and it was difficult to judge whether they were scoffing at the necking or at the loud music streaming from their radios.

To the right, a softball sailed lazily through the air. Two kids—I took them to be brothers—were having a catch. They were close to the same age, but it was clear that one of them had by far the better arm—the blond. He liked to show it off by tossing the ball high in the air. The other boy was pretty good at catching it, too. Sometimes the sun would get in his eyes and the ball would skip off his forearm or chest. It pained him for a moment, and then he was at it again. "Here's my curve ball," he shouted before letting off a toss not unlike any of the others I had seen him throw. It was one of a thousand games of catch they had shared, I was sure.

The ice cream man still shouted his mating call. "Ice cream bars. Candy bars. Three dollars. Frozen candy bars..." Three dollars. What a rip-off. I decided to take a swim. I walked toward the shoreline and removed my shirt and shoes. I delicately, stealthily, removed my gun and wrapped it in the shirt, placing all of the items about ten feet from the water's edge.

The lake was very refreshing. I felt for a moment that I was in Mother Earth's womb, ingesting her goodness through some large umbilical cord. I felt the breeze hit the back of my neck, which was now wet. It was scintillating.

From this vantage point, the whole human race didn't seem so friggin' bad after all. All of the mind-numbing hours spent waiting in line, taking orders, being pushed through the crosswalk—none of that seemed to matter anymore. I knew I had crossed a plane and that I would soon understand the state of things well beyond my years on Earth.

Even then I was feeling ideas I had never felt before. And I do mean it like I wrote it. I was *feeling* ideas. That's the only way to describe it. All of the ass-clenching we are taught here on Earth fades away, and emotion is the new prom queen. It's like nothing else you've ever experienced. The trick is to learn to harness and control those emotions—to feel your way through life like a blind man does a hallway.

An insect landed on my forearm. Rather than swat it away as I would have in the past, I allowed it to roam. I wanted to see what it would do, where it would go. It enjoyed the landscape for a minute or two, and then it lifted its wings and fluttered off into oblivion, leaving my arm unaffected by its presence. There was a real lesson in that, and I found myself admiring that tiny bug more than I ever had any human other than my wife.

Sometimes I wonder at night what it must be like to be normal. You know the type. They are born at seven and a half pounds and don't need to be delivered through the trap door up top. They just slide right out like buttered shrimp. Some kids even need to have bones broken to get their shoulders through. It's true. Especially before the C-section went and got so popular. What a way to enter the world. "Sorry, kid, you're too big." Crack!

Normal people have a talent like baseball or painting. They go to the Prom *with* someone! They play lacrosse in college. Normal people get jobs in normal fields and have two children, all healthy. If God's feeling pissed, maybe one of them will sport a cowlick. They are respected to the grave and beyond. Normal people eat corn-based cereal.

Now, to me, there's nothing normal about any of this. It's a life of clones laughing fake laughs. But the world is programmed their way, which makes it difficult for the rest of us to navigate. So we all look deviant in comparison, with our punk hairdos or our careers in speech therapy or whatever the case might be. Me? I chose population control—the good kind. I'm a border collie.

I looked toward the shore. Two children were wandering near the water's edge. The ball players. Curious little fuckers. And they were nearing my goods. Why'd they have to go and do that? It was such a very perfect and special day. I was enjoying nature, humanity. It made for a rare and lovely mix on this occasion, something that happens very infrequently indeed. And then those kids had to stop doing what they were doing and go play with the ugly man's smelly clothes.

I could see their mother calling to them. It was a slow, unconcerned call. After all, it was the ugly man's clothes, not the clothes of an executive. This man was lucky just to *have* clothes. He probably stole them. So what's the harm? Well, those clothes were more than just clothes. They were feelings. They were symbols of a man's place in the world. I still existed, damn it, and those kids were not about to deny me that.

I began to jog toward the shore.

When I was just thirty feet from the children, the mother noticed me. She stood. She screamed. And I don't mean in that "Get away from the man's clothing" wimpy voice. She screamed as if her life depended on it. Little did she know, it did.

"Franklin! Andrew! Get over here!" At first the shouting was directed at her sons. This was probably done out of politeness, to make it look as though she was concerned with her children's actions rather than my own. As I got closer, though, reality shined through her awful facade. Maybe she just saw the anger on my face and feared for her kids.

"Get away from my children! They're just playing. Get back!" She was up off her blanket now and running toward me. Damn, she was a crazy bitch! It didn't take long for her to close the distance, as she was only thirty feet from me to begin with. But that was far enough. Yes, sir, in the end, those few seconds were plenty long enough.

Chapter Thirty-Three

I grabbed my shirt from the blond boy's hand. It was light and unfettered. I looked down to the sand and saw my shoes and nothing else. There was no sign of my weapon. I went to my hands and knees and froze in place. The mother circled the three of us frantically, unsure what to do. Suddenly, I had a strange feeling. My eyes looked up very slowly.

There in front of me was a very small person holding what in *his* hands looked to be a very large gun. I will never forget that moment—and it was just a moment—for as long as I live. The child had a hand in the fate of the world. Fortunately for me, it was an uneducated and not too nimble hand.

I leaped forward at the dark-haired brat and took his forearm in my grasp. I shook his arm, and the gun fell loose to the ground. The mother had me by the other arm and screamed at the top of her lungs. What pipes she had! Mercy!

The whole scenario played out in slow motion, and the people around us were only now starting to react. Interestingly, the closer people happened to be to the action, the more slowly they appeared to move.

I waved Jill's pistol in the air in an effort to keep the people away. I felt the need for space, for breathing room. As I waved more frantically, the screaming grew more intense. People didn't know how to react, and were trapped somewhere between running and standing very, very still. It was quite a sight to behold in and of itself.

The only comparable feeling I can think of is that instant when you are at the apex of the first hill on a roller coaster. For a moment the world stands still—shiny and serene—and then you hear a buzz or a click or you feel a drop in your gut, and it's all over. I enjoyed those moments thoroughly as a child, much like I was enjoying the moment on the beach. The difference is, now *I* decided when the coaster cars would fall, when time would resume. But all good things must end.

I lowered my weapon and began taking shots. One: The bullet buzzed by an obese man. How could I miss?! Two: I hit a woman in the leg. What good would that do for me, her, or the world at large? Three: Finally! I nailed a guy—half-drunk and far too good-looking for his own good—right in the chest. His front end exploded, and he went down in a heap of ugly. Gonna need some iodine for that one, slugger. Four: I drilled a woman in a blue swimsuit. Her legs were laden with cellulite. She was ready for a diet. She wouldn't need one where she was going. She was about to catch a ferry across the River Styx.

I was running toward the road by this time. I tried to reload, but found this to be a difficult task when fleeing. People with guns aren't supposed to be fleeing, I suppose. That's the whole idea behind guns.

I wanted more, felt there was more to be done. I flung my arm back violently and took a random shot, hitting nothing but hot sand, I imagine. I wasn't actually watching, but I can only assume from the lack of intense screaming that the bullet missed any serious mark. I had to be careful now. I didn't know when I'd have time to reload, and there was only one bullet remaining to be fired. I had to conserve it. Conservation is good. Conservation is my job. Conservation of resources, of waste, of energy. Mostly conservation of waste. I'm here to conserve and preserve, actually. The people and the integrity of our planet. You don't always need to visit the Amazon to save the Earth.

Sometimes you need only go to the beach. And, hey, who doesn't like the beach? Stupid insects and whiny kids and cold water and sunburn. All of my memories seemed clouded now. Where was the good in the world? Is this all there was? My warm memories of humanity were fading as I delved deeper into my new era. I had exited my larval stage and was ready to spread my wings, but what was waiting for me beyond the world of the cocoon? Would I like it? Would *it* like *me*?

Chapter Thirty-Four

I ran, ran, ran. I don't know why I ran so far so fast. It's not like people were in any great hurry to chase down a man with a loaded weapon. Even in this age of cell phones, it would take some time to get a cruiser down there. The road appeared to be infrequently used. Besides, there was a whole world to my sides. No. I had promised myself I wouldn't take refuge in the forest once again. I should not, could not, would not, be afraid. I represented a force of bravery and strength. I had been a coward in my past life, and I could not afford to be now. I would run quickly, yes, as standing still would get me nowhere both literally and figuratively. But I would not hide.

I heard a siren and dove into the brush. What can I say? Old habits die hard.

Jill was flawed. I haven't told you that yet because I didn't want you to judge her without knowing her well. I'm running out of time now, so I have little option but to let the cat out of the bag right here and now.

Items had a bad habit of ending up in her purse, in her pockets. Nothing major, and often the items weren't even useful. Socks, butter knives, ashtrays (and neither of us smoked at the time). That kind of stuff. Now, this is a world with a name for everything. You know Jill's "condition" as kleptomania, but I don't buy all that fancy crap. Kleptomania, bulimia, bipolar, blah-blah. It's all an excuse for a healthy fee for an hourly session. My Jill was a stealin' bitch, plain and simple. I'm a smokin', drinkin', swearin' coward. She was a stealin' bitch. There are some things in life we just need to accept about each other and ourselves. Are you listening to me? Put down the bottle.

I find myself wondering if she really was such a hot toddy. Maybe I just convinced myself of that because I needed to feel loved and wanted. I mean, I never saw all the other guys looking over at her. Maybe she was an ugly slut who wanted attention. And maybe

I didn't care that she was ugly. Maybe I felt empowered because of it. I dunno, though. She looked pretty hot to me; there's no getting around that. The woman was sex personified. She was the Madonna/whore we all seek. Perhaps I was given too much in this instance. Jesus, couldn't you spread out the luck a little bit?

Jill's little problem bothered her. She swore she would just zone out in a store, a hotel, a bus station. The items would make their way into her bag or under her jacket quite without her conscious help. Now, I wouldn't have bought this line of bullshit from anyone except Jill. "Oh, I swear, Officer, I didn't even realize I was stabbing my grandma 47 times. Honest." But I trusted Jill. I tried to help her, kind of. Personally, I found her little secret to be quite dirty, sexy even. As far as I knew, it was the only truly dirty habit she had. And as far as I was knew, I was the only one who was aware of it. Talk about a turn-on.

I loved to talk to Jill about it, to tease her about it. She would hush me, embarrassed. Every once in a while, I would take the teasing too far and she would whisper, "Quiet, Edward." She could have taunted me for my own flaws, which are many and obvious. But, no, she only whispered her dissatisfaction. I had enough respect for this fact that I always respected her wishes. After one incident with some stolen cookware, Jill was in tears.

This all happened about ten years ago. I told her that her little habit wasn't so bad. She stole my heart, and my life had been all the better since. She smiled at that, and kissed me. I can still feel that kiss; truly, I can. I wonder still why she married me. Had she lost a bet? Maybe the world just figured it owed one to old Ed Caine. The way I figure it, the world owes me a lot more than a sexpot of a wife after all the shit it's thrown at me.

Chapter Thirty-Five

I've been drinking tonight (don't tell, snuck it) it's not even worth trying.

Chapter Thirty-Six

I was on the road, in an old American tradition of following a dream. I was working for all the bullied people, for all the disadvantaged folk, for every dirty, down-and-out, prejudged, not-approved-for-credit fucker who roams this Earth. I was the great equalizer, second cousin to death himself. My gun was my scythe, and my T-shirt my cloak. It was an old story updated for a **BIGGER, BOLDER, FLASHIER** new millennium. Buy now, pay later. Some assembly required. Void where prohibited.

The world was crumbling around me. Lawsuits filed friend against friend. Four-page, multi-signature, trilingual contracts to take your skis on a mountain. Need to rent? That's another contract. Everything requires directions, submissions, or releases. You almost need a lawyer in order to wipe your ass. The very freedoms our ancestors fought so bravely to assure us, are being taken away by... us!

There are advertisements on outfield walls, on mountainsides, everywhere you could conceive. Christ, if it were cost-efficient there would be a big fucking billboard for "X" beer splashed across the moon. It would blink each night in neon lights: "Drink X." Dark. "Drink X." Dark. "Drink X." Dark. And lovers would be left looking at it from lake front shores for eternity.

People with pink hair are scoffed at. They're either freaks or they're trying too hard. At least they're trying while the rest of us feel content to live in an alarm-clock world, where smog-filled streets must pass for a breath of fresh air, and where the warm glow of the sun has been replaced by sterile, humming fluorescent light.

Where's the humanity? And that's just it. The humanity was in me. If people had lost their will to find it within themselves, well, I would help them find it, or die trying. The chance for a better human existence lay, ironically, at the end of my gun's barrel. Addition by subtraction. It was time to tip the scales.

> *From Tigris and Euphrates to Madison and Park,*
> *the place might change, but we're still strangers in the dark.*
> *Start in fluid, end in dirt, confusion in between,*
> *It's time we end the madness, leave the grisly scene.*
> *Take my hand, my naive hand, admit we've gone to seed,*
> *Humans great in theory, despicable in deed.*
> Indeed.

I kind of like it. It's the closest thing to art I've ever produced. Even if it does rhyme. La, la, la, la. Big tit? Eat shit! Mwa ha ha ha.

We all have something to hide. *Short. Fat. Poor. Acne. Herpes. Dentures. Scars. Warts. Hairy nipples. Drugs. Liquor. Bad breath.* Two hours in the bathroom trying to hide our faults, not to mention the hour at the store to get the shit to do it. And what does it get us? Lonely, unfulfilling indoor lives. Run for your life.

But wait, there's more. Right now, for a limited time, you too can be exposed to rhetoric and propaganda. Pick up your phone and call now. Operators are standing by, sucker. Or we'll call you. Anything for a credit card number.

I was walking for myself. I was walking for all the Thelma Vicaros. I was a warrior, an artist, a hero. My caste was not set in stone. No, it was fluid and malleable and, most importantly, self-created. I ran probably a mile before I came upon some houses. I reloaded my weapon and shot at mailboxes and windows and fence posts. Old women came to their door and fence posts, and I shot at them. Some I hit; some I didn't. I had a neighborhood in my grasp, and indeed the world.

Thirty minutes had passed since the beach scene. At last I heard the sirens coming up behind me, and I was mixed with both dread and relief. It was a creepy feeling, comparable in its duality to that when you are *almost* drunk. Your grasp on the world is still fairly firm, yet you are looking at it with a new perspective, seeing things differently. You wonder with your glass in your hand how you could ever think the way you do under sober circumstances. You feel friendly and open and wise. This feeling of wisdom grows within you as you continue to drink and then—CRASH—your body maxes out and you suddenly feel very, very stupid. You feel left behind in the conversation. You wish you could participate in reality once again. But you have to wait for the inevitable sickness to pass. The sickness and the sleep.

So tired.

When I heard the sirens behind me, I realized my destiny was fulfilled, my job completed, but I also realized I had maxed out. I was about to crash.

And again, I felt very much alone and all too mortal.

Chapter Thirty-Seven

Officer Catbalm asked me if I understood my rights. I told him I did. Far be it from me to disrespect a man in uniform. They had done too much for me in times past. But like I said, if you haven't seen one in a while, life's peachy.

I gave Catbalm no trouble. I tossed my gun as he pulled up, and I lay flat on the ground, arms crossed behind me. He took no chances and exited his car with his gun drawn. He was joined by another squad car.

I was taken in that day, and there's not all that much I can tell you from that time on. You're all very aware of the courtroom process. The media makes sure of it, even if you are aware in only a skewed and biased fashion.

I was booked, and there was no bail set, of course. Judges don't take kindly to alleged multi-murderers who are found with the weapon practically smoking in their hand.

It must be strange to be a judge, to determine fate. And think of the drawbacks. All those hours on the bench cannot be any good for their hemorrhoids. Funny little buggers hemorrhoids are. I remember the first time I bled; I thought I was dying. My doctor told me as long as the blood was fresh and wet, I'd be okay. It's the dry stuff that's the problem. God rest his soul. Died young at 50: colon cancer. Dr. Hilbram was a good man. Just not a very good doctor. Not like you, friend.

I slept well in the cell. There was no chance for me to reconsider suicide. They make sure of that, the bastards. You'd have to run your head into the wall hard as you could. Not a pleasant option. I've heard of people chewing through their wrists, but you know what? I don't think I could hate a place that badly. I'm more of a passive suicidal. I'll take one for the team, but only a nice off-speed pitch to the buttocks.

Dr. Hilbram recommended surgery, but I decided not to do it. What's life without a little discomfort?

Why not gather a little moss, my Grandma used to ask as she sang show tunes to me in my bed. Wow, it's dark in here. And my Grandmother is not here to sing to me—she with the sagging breasts and the mismatched shoes.

Sleep.

Chapter Thirty-Eight

The death sentence. I thought it was a good idea. I would have voted for it, had they run such an election, straight up on the issues. And that's the way it should be, I think. Pull the right lever if you prefer big business, left lever if you're more environmentally conscious. If business won, we'd rip out every tree in the nation at the roots and be done with it. There's too much wishy-washiness in the world today. Too many namby-pambies. Less say, more do. Also, let's get rid of traffic lights for a day. Traffic lights and speed limits. Let's make it *fun*.

I wonder where they all are. I wonder where the other one-percenters are. What methods have they developed to carry out their mission? Somehow I felt humbled by the fact that my own efforts were so minimal. A chimpanzee can fire a gun, for crying out loud. Where was the drama, the intrigue, and the creativity you'd expect from one of your own?

Now the tide turned, and mine was the death sentence. It's different on this side. Now *you're* the executioner, Doctor. You're the judge, the jury, the butcher, the baker. You have all the parts. The unfindable actor. It sure makes you think more clearly, death row does.

Suddenly all of the red and black scrawl on the calendar has no meaning. There are no appointments and birthdays and health hazards to stress you out. It's really quite soothing knowing you're going to die *when you know you can do nothing about it*. Cancer? Heart disease? I wouldn't wish them on anybody. 'Cause there's always a chance, a hope. There's always a chance that you're *just missing* the cure. That you might live. You want to squeeze all the life that you can out of life.

Here it's different. Nothing I might say or do has any chance of saving me. I can say anything I want to say without repercussions. Like I said, you can't die twice and you only live once. It's actually quiet peaceful. I feel like I'm in a very special Hall of Fame, where entry requires only extreme hideousness. In that regard, I didn't deserve the honor to be bestowed upon me. I was no evil bastard. I was just Joe Regular who happened to be given a very special task to complete. I wasn't about to tell them that and spoil their little death party. Why leave them feeling guilty?

I know what you're thinking, you son of a bitch. It first occurred to me when I started all this, and it is still eating me up inside. I realize the nature of my words thus far. The truth is, this world is not all rainbows and butterflies, although those are very nice parts of it. Rather, the world can be a dark and pragmatic place. Within all that pragmatism, I had a purpose, and my purpose involved death.

So, yes, I know what you're thinking, and you're wrong, Doctor. I did not kill my Jill. As I said, that was the work of a man with an accountant's name. There is so little light in here, it is difficult to write this. That was the work of a man with an accountant's name. Ed Caine is no accountant. Ed Caine is no killer.

It would have been easy to murder my wife. But my wife was raped, and I wouldn't have raped her, as there would be no cause for that. I had no power issues with the love of my life. She usually let me have my way in the first place; she was very giving. Now I feel like a prick for that. Anyway, she had married me, so she must have felt *something* for me. Although that might be a debatable assumption in today's society.

People marry for riches and status and all that crap. It's all so empty, really. I don't know what's wrong with them. You. Me. Us. We're all just (by)products of what's around us. I don't know if we have no control over the world or if we have total control and just fucked it all up somewhere along the way. I don't know which is worse.

But it *would* have been easy for me to kill her. At the time of her death, the police were already all over Simmons [sic]—if not in name, at least in profile. I spelled it wrong to show you how obnoxious that little [sic] symbol is. There was so much evidence against him. If I had killed Jill before Simons got there, the police would still have assumed it to have been his handiwork.

Had I murdered her like he murdered his bitches, the police never would have thought twice. I'm sure of that. They didn't exactly pore over the murder site as it was. I told you so. I could have taken her. I admit that, for I have no reason to lie. They can add on life sentences, but they can't add on death sentences. I have only one life to give, as I had but one life to live. (Pretty faces and shallow, wanton desires) The thoughts are coming furiously now.

I think it's time to shave. Ha. ha, ha. Like I got a straight edge lying around here. I fucking wish, so that I could leave your ass here. This was fun at the start, but now I'm just pissed off and want to get it over with. Give me a straight edge, damn it! And make it a double.

Fuck math! Fuck routine! Fuck "trying to figure it all out." Fuck waiting in the doctor's office and having your teeth crowned and writing the same checks this month that you did the last and fuck nine-lame-song sets on the radio and cloudy beach days and bacon fat in my egg and cheese and fuck having to visit 'cause it's a relative and fuck ties—in sports and on necks— and fuck those little dogs-in-purses that only exist in Manhattan and fuck _____. That one I'll leave blank for your name. Fuck you.

Chapter Thirty-Nine

It's getting rather warm in here, warden. It's always so goddamn warm. Would you mind turning down the heat? To which he would no doubt reply, "Son, where you're going, there's heat enough for everybody and his brother. Get used to it." To which I would rebut, "Warden, sir, king of kings, I was righteous in my intent. If your books limit your understanding of the truth, rewrite the books. It's easier than changing the world to suit what's written within." And he would smile and drink his cold coffee. I don't trust people who prefer cold coffee. Cold coffee or warm beer.

Warm beer.

Beer.

Bee.

The bees are doing their waggle. They're pointing the way and laying the eggs. Stupidity is nature's medium. The few fight the many. We have neither numbers nor irrationality on our side. The night will be especially dark.

The warden. I only wish I had the chance to meet him for real. If I was alone with him in a dark alley, I wouldn't kick his ass. That'd be letting him get off easy. Instead I would teach him as much as I could about goodness and kindness and love. Because the more you love and feel, the more you realize how hateful the world is.

There's nothing you can do to change this, though we'd never let our kids hear us say so. And the realization that you cannot create change is punishment far beyond the liquids he will have injected into my vile, timeworn veins. When you realize that the world is not as you once saw it, with rainbows and recess and field trips, you want for your skull to crack open and your brains to leak out onto the sidewalk and fry up like a side of bacon. Then you could really enjoy life. It's all the thinking that brings us down. Blessed are the ignorant.

The time is coming, and the buzzing is nearly driving me mad. But I can sleep easily tonight knowing one thing: I didn't kill my wife. God as my witness. "God" is so close to "good." What hogwash. If we were truthful, we'd call him Meenbasterd. Could you imagine shouting *that* out during sex?

I never was a big eater, and I certainly haven't upped my intake in jail. Institution. Situation. Calibration. Infatuation. Fascination. Masturbation. Elaboration. I'll deny you the latter. I told you of the loneliness which invades our lives from time to time. Well, now is one of those times. For now you have caught up with me. I am writing this real time. And I'm doing it essentially alone. It's an awful feeling living in the present.

I think of Charles McIntyre. "Crazy Chuck." I bet he's in a better place than I am. Where's the justice in that? Screwy fucker never did a damn thing to help the world. All he did was light a fire. His mind is mush. It must be fun, such blissful ignorance. I need a break. Please remember, it's not the shark's fault that it must feed. Blame your god.

What scares you, Doctor? And why do you turn your head? Do you think your money and degrees and carefully constructed circle of friends will help to protect you? That's why we do it, you know. We build our lives to help us forget our fears in the great beyond. But when you go to sleep, Doctor, you are nothing but human. And so I ask you once again, bitch, what scares you?

Chapter Forty

I know what you're thinking. It's been a long time since last we spoke. They really take their time with this death process. What's the rush, I suppose? They have me right where they want me. Soon I will be no more than a name in a file filled with paperwork, most of which was typed up by some lonely intern in some lonely city. It's always the same. Despite our individual claims to fame, in the end we're just a name. We're all just names and addresses on forms in doctor's offices and car dealerships across this great nation. Yup, they're playing with me like a cat and its chewed-on mouse.

Death is a bad thing for those who were successful in life. For the rest of us—the majority of us—it is a new leaf. I could use one of those. I remember as a teenager wishing I could peel off my skin and remove all of the warts, the scars, the pimples that accumulate during a lifetime. Now I wish I could do the same with my soul. I am dirty. I was nature's bitch. Her little ten-dollar whore, which is more than most can venture to say. *Ten-dollar whore skippin' rope on the corner. When AIDS shows up, who's gonna mourn her? Not I, said the man with the dripping right eye, I'll rob her, and leave all you suckers to cry.*

There isn't much light in here. There isn't much light out there. Somehow I don't imagine there's much light where I'm going. I don't know why I'm talking to you, Jill. I have better things to do with my time, even here. I just have to wait for another pill. I sure hope they kill me before I get to finish this nonsense. I want to screw you one last time.

Chapter Forty-One

(Like 40, but more so!)

I'm better today.

I remember when I was young—maybe twelve years old—I went for a walk with my Granddaddy. He was a tall man and seemed immense to me at the time. This was before he was dead.

We were getting ice cream at Bartholomew's, over on Spring Street, by the record store. I remember he got vanilla, while I opted for Rocky Road. I thought his was such a silly choice. Why would anyone get vanilla when there are sweeter and more interesting choices? I suppose the question applies to more than just ice cream.

The answer reveals itself over time. Eventually we lose our sweet tooth and find enjoyment in the understated and non-complicated. At some point we realize that simplicity can be the greatest gift life has to offer. It is predictable and comforting and exceedingly rare. Binges are wild and welcome from time to time, but they often leave us feeling hollow and confused. At the end of the day, I'd gladly take a vanilla cone; I'd sure love one now.

That day, the day we went for cones, Granddaddy and I passed a beautiful woman on the street. Now, this was about the time in a boy's life when he begins to take notice of such things. She was probably twenty and had a firm, lean body. And big tits. This was before I learned about the perkies. *Some tits bounce and some tits lay; some tits got 'em growing back, back the wrong way.* Inverted nipples. Nature is comically cruel.

I noticed men on the street were ogling as well. The attention afforded the woman was something else indeed. I spoke to Granddaddy hesitantly, softly.

"It must be great to look like that."

I wasn't an attractive kid. Few ugly adults were. Granddaddy was no beauty himself, but I'll never forget his words.

"Eddie (he was the only one who called me that), there goes the most miserable creature you'll ever see." I didn't ask him at that time why he said that. I don't think it really registered there on the street. I did, however, ask him later in life. He couldn't recall the incident, for by that time he was into his seventies, but he did offer a guess as to his thinking that day outside the ice cream parlor. He told me that the people who had it worst in this world are beautiful women and rich men. Neither will know, ever, if they are truly loved.

Granddaddy died a long time ago, and is resting in grave 34N at Allpines Cemetery as I write this, but I carry his words with me in my head to this day. I realize now that one thing I can be assured of is that Jill did in fact love me. She had nothing to gain by faking it. I can only hope that she knew that my love was real, too, but I suppose that isn't the case. She was, after all, a beautiful woman. Granddaddy was a very wise man. He would have made a very good one-percenter. I sure hope he's at peace somewhere.

When you look back at your life and calculate the time you've spent sleeping or eating or tying your shoes even, it's amazing we ever have the time to get anything done. We are all taught the accomplishments of those in the past, and with each generation, the list of people past grows longer, and we are forced to leave out some of the details. Eventually we are forced to omit more and more history, meaning that there are brilliant artists and writers and thinkers that the world has long forgotten. It makes you wonder if it's worth getting up in the morning.

Time might heal all wounds, but it leaves scars in the process, and it serves to erase your existence. You might make someone smile today, but chances are good they won't remember you for very long. It's a transient world, to be sure. They say what comes around goes around, but only a fool buys into this. We are but mortal men with immortal dreams, and that is a dangerous and frustrating combination.

I am nearly to death-day. There is one more story I'd like to share before it arrives. Jill and I had been dating about six months at the time, which means we married just three months later. This was the day I realized that what I felt for Jill wasn't puppy love or infatuation or anything like that. We had rented a canoe and were traversing a river, the name of which I can no longer remember. It might have been Myers River, but I don't think so. I'm sure it wasn't the Hudson.

We were eating sandwiches out there in the middle of the river. It wasn't much of a river, actually, not like Darien's. The current was very weak. I asked her if she'd like to take a dip after lunch. After all, we were both wearing shorts and it seemed like the natural thing to do. Jill then informed me she had never learned to swim. I was surprised it hadn't come up before. There were no life vests or floats on the boat. This wasn't the Pacific Ocean, for sure, but still I wondered how she could appear so calm.

I asked her if she was worried about the canoe capsizing or something like that, and she told me she wasn't. I asked her how this could be. Jill told me she'd rather die than not live. I liked her attitude, for sure, but why not bring a life vest, just in case?

And she said, "Why have the loops in roller coasters? Why not just sit in the car on a hard, steel track? You have to get the most for your four dollars." It might not seem like much of a statement, and the analogy is hackneyed for certain, but it did more to convince me that we were meant to be together than did her beauty and smarts and humor all rolled together. If you don't understand that, you've never been in love.

I realize now that I haven't been in full control in quite a while. I find that my thoughts are more and more muddled. I'm not sure if this is because of the drugs or if my mind is just growing tired. Waiting for death can be quite exhausting.

Maybe they are slipping me something to keep me quiet. A man on death row has nothing to lose. Maybe they're afraid that somehow this little man will find a way to take out a guard who would do well in professional football. I suppose the pills are paid for with tax revenue. In that case, why not spread them around?

Chapter Forty-Two

My time is now. I have waited an eternity, it seems, and today is the day. I am looking forward, as you might expect. Now is the time when I go to a better place and learn that I was right.

It is a gray day, which I assume is only appropriate. At least the Good Lord provided a proper setting. I came in with nothing, and that's all I have now. I am fortunate to have somebody to help me with this each day. They will not afford me a pencil. I suppose I could take out an eye with it if I wanted to.

It took a lot of hard work to find someone to help, and it is time now to thank him. Guilt for the damned, I suppose. I also have to thank all of those people in my life who helped me find some measure of peace in this unpredictable world. I need to thank those who I loved; you know who you are. None of that award-ceremony nonsense.

I'm not going to go out with a hissy fit, Mother; I want you to know that. I will take my medicine with dignity and honor. Not that I should, mind you. I have more than one reason to gripe. The abuse as a child. The abuse as an adult. I had to suffer through a world I didn't understand just because you and dad got the itch one night to raid your foul-smelling hole. Maybe it's not me. Maybe *you* wanted a child like some people want a dog. Someone to feed and to give shelter to and to turn to for self-assurance in a hostile world. Trouble is, I didn't always bring back the stick. Sometimes I chose to run far and wide with it. To meet other dogs and to explore. This bothered you; I know it did.

The women in my life have held me back, and the men have pushed my head beneath the surface of the water.

I don't regret what I've done, and when I'm gone, the papers will all write that I showed no remorse. Remorse for what? I ask you. For thinking on my own two feet? For trying to feel? I cannot and will not feel shame for that. I hope that after I go, the man beside me will take these papers and continue them, so that my story will be written and I will have died with purpose. I can only hope for that. Perhaps I'll even make it into come college kid's term paper.

But now it is time for me to go. I wish to enjoy my final hours in golden silence, daydreaming of high, blue skies and of better places than this, where the showers are always hot and dreams really do come true. I've been in and out of a haze for quite a while now. I know my obituary will not be a thing of beauty. It will be written by an underpaid employee at the newspaper who knows me only as a natural born killer.

I'll be labeled as "sick" or "disturbed" or some such euphemism. It won't look to explain my actions, though my lack of children might be suspected as contributing to my "illness." He'll turn his copy in to his editor and return to his home, where he will spend the rest of his days wondering how it is that he should spend his time writing about other people's lives rather than living his own. He will crawl beneath the covers of his bed at night in the thirty-dollar pair of underwear he can't afford and wonder where it all went. And one day his time will come, too, and all he'll be left with is the wish that he be remembered and the knowledge that he won't.

I really hope there is a bright light and a long tunnel. I hope God will approach me and shake my hand and order me a drink from the bar. If He should, I am sure the liquor will be stiff and the glass will be tall. I can see God as a bourbon guy. Bourbon and unfiltered cigarettes. I bet he'll wear sneakers too.

Maybe I'll meet up with all of the great minds of the past, and they will turn to me and say in unison, "You had it right." Maybe there will be a flavor better than vanilla. And perhaps, just perhaps, I'll get another crack at this world. Maybe you will too. And perhaps, just perhaps, I'll come back as *your* son or daughter. Maybe then you'll understand what true love is all about, when I look at you and you look at me and we enjoy a moment of comfortable silence.

And maybe years from now, Doctor, as I sit beside you on your deathbed far away from here, I will turn to you and say thanks for bringing me into this lovely world, and bring a smile to your face. For that is all I could ever want.

—Edward Pritchard Caine

Addendum

E dward Caine died on February 13th. He didn't quite
make Valentine's day, I am sorry to say. It was his
favorite holiday. It is my duty now, as he would have
liked, to finish the tale with the same instrument I've
been using all this time.

Edward spent the last years of his life in a
compromised mental state. From all of the evidence
I can gather, he was a good man with a big heart. In
his final days, I spent a lot of time speaking with him,
getting to know him, really. Sometimes a clouded mind
speaks the most truth. Unfortunately, his mind did
not provide for him all the years it should have been
expected to.

Edward's father was a sore subject for him, but
I feel it would help you now to know more about him.
Robert Caine was a merchant who married too young
and for all the wrong reasons. There's no need to name
them. When Edward arrived in this world, Robert
felt jealous of him. Jealous of his own son. I don't
believe Edward ever got over this fully. The guilt was
omnipresent.

Edward felt he had a lot to prove. He took to
drinking as a young man, and he left his best years
behind him as a teen. Very few people were able to see
the good in him after that time. To be truthful, very few
people saw the good in him before, from what I hear.

It is my belief that his real problems—the
problems that eventually led to his mental breakdown—
originated at the time that the Solemn Stalker was doing
his thing, back in the fall of '05. The whole occurrence
turned Edward against humanity, and who can blame
him?

He began to dwell on the limitations and flaws
of modern society. At first it led only to heavy drinking
and a fatalistic attitude, but then the element of nature
came into play. He seemed to develop a belief within
himself that he had a purpose, something that most of

us never find for ourselves. For that I give him credit.

Unfortunately, he never reached his full potential. Not by a long shot. His actions became despicable. He would curse the very people he loved. But it is my belief that he did all of this with the greatest of intentions. It was Edward's desire to shake up the world, which we must quietly admit has gathered quite a bit of dust in recent times.

Edward was given a mind which craved knowledge, and he felt alone in that cause. There was no way anyone he knew could ever understand what he was feeling, no more than we can understand what anyone is feeling on God's green Earth. Suffice it to say, he began as a simple man who had little noticeable effect on the world around him, and ended as a complex man who had just the same.

In truth, Edward never murdered anyone. Maybe now you'll understand that, if you didn't before. He fell into a spiral of self-pity where every day was a gray day in his eyes. He had, after all, only two options. He could try to fight an impossible battle—waking up the world to its own limitations—or he could fault himself. He was a good man, as I've stated, and he chose the latter, not out of laziness or incompetence, but because he realized the other would only cause pain. Pain is something he'd rather inflict on himself. And so he did.

It started mentally, creating a fantasy world where the rules were his to create, where there was reason and purpose, and where he could place the blame squarely where he felt it belonged.

Eventually, his mind suffered from it, and this had repercussions on his day-to-day existence. He lost his lust and love for life, the qualities which made such a simple man so oddly admirable to begin with. At last, I presume, he found it just wasn't worth the effort anymore.

I found his body on a Friday; that much I remember. The worst part about it is that, yes, it was my gun he used. And I have to live with that, always.

—Jill McIntyre-Caine

About the Author:
John W. Podgursky

John Podgursky lives in Brooklyn. He's spent the last 15 years traveling the U.S. of A., trying to make sense of it all. He's still confused, but sleeps well at night knowing that nobody else knows any better, and in the end we're just going to die anyway.

Also from Damnation Books:

 Concubine
by Geoff Chaucer
Erotica Horror
Short Story

ISBN: 978-1-61572-027-9 ebook

The Emperor finds a certain concubine very
pleasing. She studies with an old hetaera
to make herself yet more pleasing but soon
discovers that the old woman is actually in
the employ of the Empress and has something other that the sexual pleasure of the
Emperor in mind.

www.dAmnAtionBooks.com

DAMNATION
BOOKS

HORROR
DARK FANTASY
PARANORMALS
SCIENCE FICTION
THRILLERS
EROTICA

EBOOK
digitAl
TRADE PAPERBACK

CPSIA information can be obtained at www.ICGtesting.com
Printed in the USA
LVOW11s0824291113

363030LV00001B/45/P